LOVE'S PILGRIMAGE

LOVE'S PILGRIMAGE

Phyllis Caggiano

BETHANY HOUSE PUBLISHERS
MINNEAPOLIS, MINNESOTA 55438
A Division of Bethany Fellowship, Inc.

Published by Bethany House Publishers
A Division of Bethany Fellowship, Inc.
6820 Auto Club Road, Minneapolis, MN 55438

Printed in the United States of America

Library of Congress Cataloging-in-Publication Data

Caggiano, Phyllis, 1938–
   Love's pilgrimage.

   I. Title.
PS3553.A345L65   1986   813'.54   86-12895
ISBN 0-87123-808-X (pbk.)

For Gary,
whose wisdom and strength
help ease the journey.

PHYLLIS CAGGIANO, born, raised and married in Arizona, now makes a home for her husband and five children in the town of Glendale. She began writing some years ago and has had articles published in various periodicals. Research and writing for her first book, *Love's Fragile Flame*, required six years and included a visit to England for further background information and descriptions. That research was also the basis for this her second book, *Love's Pilgrimage*. She and her husband are active in the North Phoenix Baptist Church.

Chapter One

"EARTH, WATER, AIR and fire. These be the four elements of life out of which all else is made."

"Mmm?" Joan mumbled through a mouthful of pins as she hemmed Rose's wedding dress.

" 'Twas nothing," Rose replied. "Merely a saying my father taught me long ago." She sighed and continued staring into the fire in the bedchamber hearth. Earth, water, air and fire. *Which element shall have sovereignty in my life with Thomas*, she wondered. She well knew the element which reigned in her first marriage—fire. *'Twas a friendly element at first, warming the passion of first love, heating the coals in Derick's forge as he labored in his smithy in Boxton, making a cheery glow in the hearth of our cottage.*

Suddenly the log on the hearth broke and tumbled into the ashes, sending long flaming tongues up the chimney. The vision of Derick tied to the stake on Boxton green flashed into her mind. She closed her eyes. *Away, away,* she commanded the terrible memory. *I must think on pleasant matters.* She looked down at little Derry seated on the floor. He too was staring into the fire with curious, but heavy-lidded eyes. As his head dropped down, a black curl fell over his forehead just as his father's had done. *I have taken the right course. I am so lonely and Derry needs a father. Thomas is not at all like Derick except for his love for the Lord.* She thought of the four elements and wondered again which would reign in her new marriage. Earth mayhap. Thomas would be taking Derry and her to live on the manor he had recently purchased in Suffolk. What could be more earthy than plowed fields, flocks of sheep and the scent of new-mown hay? Ah, but what of water. Water had played an important part in the events that led up to her meeting Thomas. Was it not here in Joan's house, on London Bridge over the River Thames, that she had found refuge after Derick's death? And had she not traveled across the North Sea in search of her brother Robin and found not only him but Thomas as well? And did not Thomas's trade as merchant adventurer often take him across the seas? Yea, water it would be, she told herself, not realizing how apt the symbol was to prove. For water takes on many forms—the gentle meandering river ofttimes wells up into a destructive flood, and the calm surface of the sea can conceal hidden obstacles and dangerous undercurrents.

"You shall make a beautiful bride, I will say that much," Joan said as she struggled to her feet. She helped Rose out of the wedding gown and into her everyday clothes. "Derry cannot keep his eyes open," she said. "Poor lad, 'tis the last night he'll be sharing his mother's bed."

"Of a truth, Joan," Rose protested, "you speak as if 'twill be a funeral instead of a wedding tomorrow. We've—"

"Mistress, quickly!" a servant girl exclaimed as she burst into the bedchamber. "The Queen's Majesty herself. Her royal barge is being towed up and down the river. There are hundreds of other boats about and fireworks and trumpeting!"

"Our new monarch does enjoy displaying herself to her subjects," Joan said as she scooped up Derry. "Come, little sleepy head. You shall not see pageantry like this in Suffolk." She and Rose followed the servant girl into the narrow lane which separated the rows of shops and houses on London Bridge. They found an open space between two shops across the way where they could look out onto the river toward Baynard's castle. It was a fine May evening as the setting sun gilded the rippling surface of the Thames.

"I can see Queen Elizabeth seated on a throne in the middle of the barge," said the servant girl.

Joan squinted into the setting sun. "Nonsense, girl, the barge is too far down river. With all the boats hovering about it, I can scarce see its banners waving, much less make out human forms."

"I would like to see Her Majesty face-to-face one day," said Rose.

"I feel akin to her. We were both born on the seventh day of September in 1533; both unfairly imprisoned, she in the Tower and I in Newgate Prison; and God's hand delivered both of us through perilous times. I am joyed that God has blessed her with a crown and kingdom."

"Dear friend, you have endured more sorrow than she. Where is your crown and kingdom?"

Rose reached over and caressed Derry's black curls. "Here is my joy and crown. As for a kingdom, well, mine is the kingdom of the Lord Jesus Christ. By His mercy He has allowed me to dwell in it."

Joan shook her head slowly. "I marvel at your trust in God, and ofttimes"—her robust voice softened—"ofttimes I covet such belief."

"If you truly desired to believe, you would. But I know you too well, Joan Denly. You would ever rule your own kingdom."

"Hmmph. If I hadn't taken a hand in my own affairs years ago, I would be another poor widow begging on the streets or rotting away in some almshouse." She hoisted Derry on her hip and pulled herself up to her full height, towering over Rose. "I built this business up after my man died, and now there's no more prosperous mercer in all of London. I need not bow to any man—which brings me back to the morrow. Why this haste to tie yourself to a husband? And if you will insist on marrying, at least wait a bit. I can introduce you to some fine young bucks. Remember the saying, "She who marries in May shall rue the day."

Rose laughed. "You've only quoted it fifty times since the wedding bans were posted. Thomas Stratton is a fine Christian gentleman; I am a widow with a child and not a pence to my name. Besides, what would entice one of your 'young bucks' to marry me when he could have a wealthy young bride?"

"Oh, and are you so ancient at six and twenty years? Well, lady, they would be enticed by the same qualities that please your Thomas. You are a comely, intelligent woman with as fair and clever a child as ever born."

"I won't deny the latter." There was a burst of fireworks about a hundred yards downriver and Joan raised Derry up to the ledge of the stone wall for a better view. "Have a care, Joan, he'll fall into the water."

"Verily, you are a mother hen clucking over her one chick," chided Joan. "Let the child enjoy the sight. He won't be able to see fireworks in the wilds of Suffolk."

"Hardly the wilds. I've seen a sketch of the manor house, and it could easily house four of your shops, including your living quarters above. And Bury St. Edmunds, no small town, is but a few miles away." Rose patted her friend's shoulder. "I shall miss you and be forever grateful for the way you've sheltered Derry and me. You will come and visit us?"

"I'm not a traveler like that Thomas of yours, but yes, I may visit sometime. Although I'm no lover of farms and the beasts that reside on them. A glorified farm is all your grand manor is, you know."

"Nevertheless, 'twill be good for Derry to be raised where the air is wholesome," replied Rose. "I fear the plague here in London now that summer is approaching." She touched Derry's cheek. "He seems a bit feverish."

Joan put her lips to Derry's forehead. "Bah. He's a healthy lad and big for his two and half years, I'll ween."

"Aye, he shall be as tall as his father."

After a few minutes silence Joan asked, "Will you tell him what befell his father?"

"Oh, when he can bear the hearing of it and when I"—her voice broke—"when I can bear to tell him. He shall hear it all." Rose stared out across the water. The sun had disappeared and the royal barge along with the attending boats were fading into floating shadows in the distance. She thought back to her moments with Derick, just minutes before his death at the stake. She tried to recall his face, but the image faded in her memory. However, she could still remember the feel of their last embrace and the sound of his voice as he had prayed, "Father in heaven, take care of them, Rose and the babe. Be my strength this day. Let me die praising your name." God had answered his prayer. His death and the deaths of hundreds of other Protestant martyrs had been testimonies of the truth of God's Word. And the Lord had taken care of Derick's child that she had been carrying when he died. Derry had been healthy at birth, even in that miserable prison cell, and Joan's rescue of the babe had been nothing but miraculous. Now God was providing a husband for her and someone to care for Derry. How could she not tell the lad all this when he grew older? Joan's voice broke her reverie. She was rocking Derry in her arms and crooning to him.

"Poor little lamb, soon to have a strange man ordering him about."

"Thomas is not a stranger, Joan. I lived with the exiles in the English house in Emden long enough to know him well."

"Horsefeathers. You never truly know a man until you've shared his bed and board. Why, my old man used to—" She paused as the two saw Thomas approach. Although it was now twilight, they could see him clearly as he paused under a newly lit torch on the wall of a shop. He was hatless and wearing a broad-shouldered cape of dark red velvet. His light brown hair caught the glow of the torchlight. He smiled when he spotted Rose by the wall and came toward them. "A handsome dog, I'll grant you that," Joan loudly whispered.

Rose nodded and smiled. Although not tall, Thomas did have finely wrought features and moved with a manly grace, but it was the confident, kindly look about his eyes that pleased her most.

"Good evening, ladies." He nodded to Joan and gave Rose a kiss on the cheek in greeting.

"Tush, the bridegroom should not see the bride on the eve of the wedding; 'twill bring bad luck," Joan chided.

"An old wives' tale," Thomas answered without taking his eyes off Rose.

"Hmm, well, this old wife must go inside," Joan said. "I know when my presence is not desired." She started to hand Derry over to Rose but Thomas held up his hand.

"Would you be so kind as to take the lad inside with you?" he asked. "He should be abed by now."

"Oh, but there may be more fireworks and he loves them so," Rose protested.

"The lad needs his sleep," Thomas said firmly, and took her hand as he added in gentler tones, "and I desire to speak with you privately."

"Very well, Thomas. Joan, do you mind?"

Joan shifted Derry over to her other shoulder and stepped back from the couple with exaggerated motions as Derry began to cry,

"Boat, boats—I want to stay and see lights."

"There, there, dearling," Joan said as she gave him a loud thump on the back. "Master Stratton says you should be abed, and he must be obeyed even if he is not your true father."

"I pray you'll forgive Joan," Rose apologized when Joan was out of hearing. "She loves Derry and me as if we were her kin and just desires our happiness."

" 'Tis all I desire also," Thomas replied. There was a moment of awkward silence and they both turned to look out upon the darkening river. Finally Thomas cleared his throat and said, "All is in readiness for the wedding feast. My cook informed me she spent the day running from shop to marketplace procuring divers dainties to feed our guests. Oh, forgive me, dear. I should have had her consult with you about the food."

"Nay, Thomas, I have never entertained gentry. I would die of fright if I had to do it on my own. As it is, I fear I will embarrass you before your guests."

"*Our* guests," he said as he took her hands, "and you could never embarrass me." He was standing so close to her, she wished that he would take her in his arms and kiss her as Derick would have done, no matter how many people were about. But he wasn't Derick, and she told herself that she must stop expecting him to behave as Derick would. Thomas was more controlled, more formal in public, as a gentleman should be. Besides, since his proposal the month before, they had scarcely been alone together for more than a few moments at a time. He had made two trips to the Suffolk manor, and the rest of the time he had been occupied with his business. He had devoted the last five years to meeting the needs of the exiled Protestants who had fled England and Queen Mary's persecution. Now he had to reestablish his contacts with English clothmakers and revive his foreign trade. *Once we are married and away from the city, we will be more at ease with each other*, she thought.

"I have a little gift for you," Thomas said, "but the light is dimming and I fear you cannot see it."

"We could go into Joan's house," she suggested.

"Nay, I wish to show it to you privately. Here, stand in the torchlight." He pulled out a little leather pouch and turning his back so as to shield the object from the view of passersby, he held it out to her. It was a ruby the size of a robin's egg encased in gold filigree.

"How beautiful!" she exclaimed, but she drew her hand back when a sudden thought occurred to her. "Was it—I mean, did it belong to—?"

"This stone was my mother's. My father acquired it from a Spaniard who claimed it came from China and may have belonged to the royal family there. I did present it to Audrey after we wed, but she never wore it. She had many jewels of her own and thought this stone too crudely wrought. I think its rich history gives it an added beauty that other jewels do not possess. That's why I wanted you to have it. Aud—er—others could not appreciate its true value."

Rose accepted the ruby with child-like excitement and turned it in her hand, allowing it to shimmer in the torchlight.

" 'Tis lovely indeed," she murmured. "I will cherish it also because it belonged to your mother. And Thomas, never fear to mention Audrey's name to me. I cannot help but speak Derick's name now and then. After all, his son shall always bear his name. We cannot pretend our first mates never existed. We wouldn't wish to. I know you must have loved Audrey very much."

He looked embarrassed. "I—I was fond of her. It was an arranged marriage, planned to strengthen both our families' holdings in the cloth market. I traveled much and she was in ill health most of the time, but uncomplaining of her fate. Still, she looked well to the household and made our manor in Kent a pleasant place to return to. I know you, too, must have been quite fond of your husband."

Fond, she thought. *Fond? How can I tell you that he was my love, my life. Oh, poor Thomas, you've never known what true married love can be. The passionate love that binds two people together as a grafted branch is bound to a vine until the two truly grow as one. I was blessed to be one with Derick. Oh, Father,* she silently prayed, *help me to love and cherish this dear man as I should.*

Chapter Two

"ROSE, MY DEAR, the manor is but a few more miles," Thomas called over his shoulder. The path between hedgerows was narrow and there was just room for their horses to travel single file. "We could rest for a bit if you wish."

"Nay, let us go on," she replied. The thought of having to dismount and mount again distressed her more than staying in the saddle. This three-day journey on horseback had been her first riding experience in years, and although it became increasingly more uncomfortable, she was glad she rode. Following the narrow paths through woods and pastures was far more interesting than lumbering along on the supply wagons that followed wider roads. She heard Derry laugh and glanced back at him. He was chattering happily to the manservant who rode with him on a staid old mare.

Thomas had paused to break off a branch of hawthorn that hung across the path. He handed the mass of white flowers back to her with his quick, shy smile and spurred his horse ahead. *He cannot wait to show me our new home*, she thought fondly. She was grateful he had purchased the manor for them instead of taking her to his estate in Kent where he had lived with his first wife. Rose's horse lost his footing slightly and jostled her in the saddle, making her more uncomfortable. To pass the time she thought back to her wedding day one week earlier.

They had been married in the ancient church of St. Dunstain in the East, and had returned to Thomas' large house on Thames Street. Conveniently near the Custom House in Tower Street Ward, it stood very close to London Bridge. Rose thought it a fair house, for though its ground floor consisted of a counting room and large storage rooms for wool, silk and other trade goods, the living quarters above were spacious and finely furnished.

The wedding feast had been attended by members of the Merchant Adventurers and their wives along with several of the Protestant clergy, who, like Thomas, were newly returned from exile. Rose had felt ill at ease around Thomas' business acquaintances and so stayed close by his side as he spoke with a small group of the clergy.

"I must say I am disappointed in the stand taken by Her Majesty, or should I say the lack of a stand against all traces of Catholicism," one minister was saying.

Another answered, "But one can see why she does not intend to anger either side until her position is secure."

"You would speak thus, Cox," retorted the first. "Rumor has it that Queen Elizabeth will soon appoint you Bishop."

"I pray 'twill be so," said Cox.

"How can you compromise your beliefs after the deaths of so many martyrs to the Protestant cause, besides the years we've all spent in exile?"

"We must be practical," Cox replied. "I myself am older and not so much of a hot fanatic as I once was."

"Hot? Nay, you never came near the flames."

Rose had sighed loudly in spite of herself. *Some men will ever argue their religion while others lay down their lives for their beliefs,* she thought.

"Gentle sirs, have a care," came a voice from behind her. "You are boring this lovely bride to tears with your dry theology."

While the two debaters muttered replies, Rose turned around to see the speaker. She almost gasped when she saw a young man about twenty whose resemblance to Derick was quite uncanny. He had the same unruly black hair and broad shoulders. But as she studied his features more closely, she could see that in spite of similarities about the nose and eyes, he had a softer jawline and weaker mouth than her first husband. Still, his appearance had startled her.

"Rose," Thomas said as he clapped a hand on the young man's shoulder, "allow me to present my new assistant, Edmund Laxton.

His father sponsored my first trading venture, and now I've taken Edmund in hand to teach him all I know about foreign trade."

Edmund had bowed and with an appraising smile on his face had said, "Of a truth, Thomas, you must also teach me how to win so comely a bride and I shall forever be in your debt."

Thomas had to smile at Rose as he replied, "My pardon, Edmund, but that I cannot do. It was the Lord who found her for me."

The rest of the evening's festivities had been a blur to Rose. She remembered how awkwardly she had replied to polite questions. The women, especially the merchants' wives, had been openly curious about her. " 'Tis good to see Thomas back in London," said one bejeweled matron. "Why he chose to go abroad and spend his substance on housing a ragtag group of religious fanatics is beyond my comprehension."

"Mayhap Audrey's death had unsettled his mind somewhat," said another as she tapped her head with an ivory fan.

"Well, I'm joyed that all this bother about religion is done with," said the first. "In the last year of Queen Mary's reign, one couldn't pass Smithfield on market day without seeing some heretic roasting."

Rose had just stared at the women, her mind searching for the proper words to say. Her face must have revealed her shock and anger, for both of the women had hurriedly stepped away to join another circle of conversation. For a moment Rose had regretted Joan's decision not to attend the wedding feast but to stay home and care for Derry. Her outspoken friend would have had words aplenty to reply to those callous remarks.

When the last guest had departed, Rose recalled how Thomas had laughed self-consciously as he surveyed the dining hall. " 'Tis over and done with. How merrymakers can eat! I thought Sir Maynard would surely expire from a surfeit of roast pigeon."

She smiled at him and his eyes held her glance. Then he looked down and picked up a silver-gilt wineglass that had been overturned, leaving a crimson circle on the white linen tablecloth.

"More drink? or meat?"

She shook her head, embarrassed at her sudden shyness. A maid-servant holding a large tray hesitated in the doorway. Thomas motioned for her. "Beatrix, show Mistress . . . *Stratton*"—he emphasized her new name—"to the great bedchamber." The little maid curtsied and took a candlestick from one of the dining tables. "I'll just see to the locking up and join you presently," he told Rose.

The great bedchamber's chief furnishing was a huge canopied bed with coverings of cream colored silk. Rich tapestries adorned every wall and a small fire was glowing in the tiled hearth. As Rose had changed into her nightgown, she couldn't help comparing the room to the small bedchamber in the cottage at Boxton where she and Derick had shared their wedding night and all the nights for six years until the sheriff's men had come to arrest him for his new-found faith in Christ. *Cease. Cease,* she told herself. *God has given me a new life, a new husband and*—there was a soft tap on the bedchamber door and Thomas had entered—"

"Rose."

Her reverie was broken by Thomas calling to her ahead on the path. The path had widened and she rode up to the top of the small hillock and looked where Thomas was pointing. She saw a small thoroughfare village of thatched cottages and timber-framed shops with jettied stories above. In the distance, behind a stand of ash trees, she could see the flint church tower. "That's the village of Good-thorpe. Our manor is beyond." He swept his hand across the landscape before them.

"Just how large is the manor?" she asked.

" 'Tis about 1900 acres, all told, including pasture, meadows, and woods."

She shook her head wonderingly. "That one man could own so much property."

"One man and his wife," he said. "All that I possess is yours also." He reached over and patted her hand. "Beside, most of it is let out to tenants. Just as the former owner, I've chosen to retain a few hundred acres for our own use. Now come, let me show you the Hall."

As they rode through Goodthorpe, Rose noticed several people staring out the windeyes of cottages as they passed by. A mother rushed out to grab up her little girl as she ran toward the horses. The woman curtsied to Rose with the child in her arms, and several men in front of the smithy doffed their caps. It all made Rose feel as if she were playing the part of the queen in a May Day pageant.

As they rode past the village and down a lane bordered by a thick hedgerow, she caught a glimpse of red-bricked turrets rising above a row of elms. "What is that place, Thomas, a castle or an old abbey?"

He laughed. "Nay, my whiting, 'tis Grendal Hall, our new home."

They turned into the drive which ran under the ornamental iron arches of a wide gate and approached the courtyard which faced away from the lane and toward wide fields of corn. Viewing the Hall from the back she would see a stately garden and ornamental shrubbery fringing the three-storied building. "Oh, Thomas!" she exclaimed, " 'tis too grand a dwelling for the likes of me."

But as they turned toward the courtyard, giving her a full view, she could see the many outbuildings lying just beyond. There was a dairy with vats set out to dry. Farther on behind a stand of poplars, she could make out stables and a chicken house. In the courtyard itself there were several old roosters scratching the ground. She even saw a little pink house pig nuzzling the leg of a maidservant who was busily rendering fat in a large kettle near the Hall's entrance. At the end of one foot of the E-shaped courtyard stood a huge dovecote, with doves flapping their wings, scattering feathers over the ground.

Rose smiled. At least Joan had been right about one thing. This grand manor was nothing but a large farm. Since Rose had grown up on her aunt's small farm outside of Boxton, she felt she would be more at home here than in the townhouse in London.

"I've kept the servants on," Thomas was saying. "Humfrey the overseer assures me they are all good workers, most of them born and raised in these parts. There are several women of the village who come in to help with the laundry, and so forth." He dismounted and helped her down. She turned to help Derry, but he was already off the horse and chasing the squealing little pig.

The next few weeks passed quickly and happily. Rose was relieved to find that the household ran smoothly without any specific orders from her. Bess, the short, pear-shaped cook, ran a tight kitchen, and Thomas seemed pleased enough with the food served. The housework was supervised by Sybil, a red-headed maid. She had large, red hands which she continually wiped with her apron. Her watery eyes and thin lips, drawn in a permanent expression of disapproval, made Rose grateful she was not one of her maidservants. The woman's saving grace was her immediate fondness for Derry. On that first day she took charge of the boy, carrying him up to the small bedchamber next to theirs, which would be his nursery.

It was sheep-shearing time. Thomas, Rose and Derry watched the shepherds wash the sheep in the stream which ran through the estate. Derry loved to watch the shearers after he was assured that the sheep were unharmed by the process. Thomas enjoyed playing the gentleman farmer, while Humfrey's face grew more long-suffering each day. In the afternoon, Thomas, Rose and Derry would go riding. Although Derry would usually fall asleep in Thomas's saddle, Rose refused to leave him in Sybil's care while they rode.

Her concern for Derry caused the one unhappy time in every day. Each night as Rose put him to bed in his nursery, he cried to be allowed to sleep with her. One evening when she had finally put him to bed, he followed her to her bedchamber and clung to her skirts, sobbing, "I want to sleep with you, Mama."

Rose looked at Thomas, already in bed. "Just this once?" she pleaded.

"Nay," he answered firmly. "The lad must learn to sleep in his own room. We want to raise a man, not a mother's boy." With a sigh, she picked up the crying child and carried him back to his own bed, but she crawled in beside him and lay there until he fell asleep. When she finally slipped back into her own bed, Thomas muttered something into his pillow.

"What, dear?" she asked. He didn't answer but turned away from her. *Verily, he's jealous of my love for Derry*, she realized. *How dare*—she stopped herself and turned toward him, lightly placing her hand on his shoulder. *'Tis proof he truly loves me, and Thomas, I am growing to love you,* she thought and inched closer until her body was barely touching his. He remained stiffly on his side for a few moments and then turned and embraced her.

The next morning as they sat at breakfast, Sybil returned from answering the door and announced, "A gentleman—come to call on Master Stratton." Thomas went into the parlor to receive him and soon returned grinning. "Well, my dear, you might be looking at the next Commissioner of Peace for Suffolk County. That was Squire

Mortimer. I met him when I purchased the manor. Apparently there is a vacancy and he wants to submit my name at the next session." He chuckled. "Wouldn't my old vagabond sire be surprised to know his son might become a Justice of the Peace?"

"I'm proud of you, Thomas."

"There's just one matter. I hope you won't mind, but I was so joyed at Mortimer's words that I invited him and his wife to dinner tonight."

"Tonight, but what will I—"

"I'm certain the cook can manage," he said hastily. "There's really no need for you—" but Rose was halfway out of the room, her brain teeming with tasks and details. This would be her first social event as lady of the manor, and she wanted to make Thomas proud of her.

Bess reassured her. "Have no care. I shall prepare a fine meal." But as the day wore on she presented Rose with a parade of discouraging remarks. First it was, "Forget about a first course. There's no fish but some salt cod that I couldn't serve to the swineherder." Then she warned, " 'Twill be naught but plain roast meats. I haven't time to grind beef for pumpes or allowes and besides, there are no nuts for the almond milk," and finally, "Tarts are done, but they're not my best."

Rose wished she could take over the kitchen and cook up a simple pottage and serve it with a coarse loaf, but of course such a meal would offend their guests. Instead, she busied herself selecting the best linen cloths from the napery and requested the chambermaid to search for the set of gilt spoons Joan had given her as a wedding gift. By midafternoon she had a terrible headache and a great desire to hide in the hayloft until her guests had departed.

Rose tried on several gowns before she chose an old ivory silk. As she was musing on her choice, there was a knock on the bedchamber door and Sybil entered. "May I assist you, madam?" she asked. "I am skilled at dressing hair."

Rose started to refuse. She had never become accustomed to servants helping her with her personal care, but she did want Thomas to be proud of her appearance. She nodded and held her head stiffly as Sybil first brushed her hair and then began to braid it into an intricate design. After a moment the maidservant stood back to inspect her handiwork. "If you have some pearls, I could intertwine them on these braids like a crown."

"Oh, but I hardly think—very well." Rose unlocked her jewel casket and brought out a single strand of pearls.

"Aye, those will do nicely and, if I may suggest, your gown lacks color. Mayhap some bright jewels?"

"I know just the thing," Rose said. Lifting the false bottom from the casket, she pulled out the magnificent ruby broach Thomas had given her and held it to the neckline of her gown. "Will this do?"

Sybil's eyes riveted on the ruby, and it was some time before she answered, "What?—Oh, aye, madam, 'tis wondrous fair. May I?" She almost grabbed the broach and lovingly stroked it with her large reddened hand as she said softly, "Even I would be comely wearing such a jewel as this."

Later when Thomas came up to change for dinner, he bowed low when he saw Rose. "Your Majesty," he said in mock-serious tones, "I had no idea that royalty would grace our table tonight." He took her hand with a flourish and kissed it.

Rose pulled back her hand and patted her hair anxiously. "Oh, Thomas, are you saying I am overdressed? I could take out these pearls and—"

"Nay, dearling," he laughed. "You are the lady of the manor, and the fairest one, I'll ween, in all Suffolk County. I'm certain the squire's wife will seem but a shadow beside you."

In spite of Bess's dire pronouncements, she served a good substantial meal. The squire ate with relish and although his wife daintily cut her food in small portions and ever so gently speared them with her knife and slipped them into her mouth, still she managed to clean the platter of roast doves. The squire did most of the talking during the meal, and when Thomas took him off to see his plans for enlarging the house, Mistress Mortimer leaned across the table and asked, "What was your maiden name, dear?"

"Allworth," Rose replied.

"Of the Colchester Allworths?"

"Nay. London."

Mistress Mortimer laughed. "I could have sworn I heard—ah

well, 'tis strange how false information gets bandied about. Do you know that my chambermaid heard someone swear that you were once a prisoner in Newgate Prison and that your son was actually born—''

Rose stood up abruptly. "Speaking of my child, I must see if he is asleep. Please excuse me." Her cheeks were flaming as she went upstairs.

She had given Derry a light meal of bread and cheese before their guests had arrived, and he had fallen asleep eating it. She was concerned that he might wake up still hungry, but when she entered the nursery he was nowhere in sight. She dashed to her own bedchamber but it was empty. "Sybil, Sybil!" she called down from the gallery.

"Yea, madam?" the maid held a tray of dishes.

"Has Derry wandered down to the kitchen?"

When she shook her head Rose ordered her to go up and search the servants' quarters while she searched below. "Rose, what is amiss?" Thomas met her at the foot of the stairs. When she told him he enlisted the squire's aid and soon the house, garden and courtyard had been thoroughly searched. "He must have slipped out the door into the garden," Rose said, her voice rising with panic. "Remember, we left it open after we showed the Mortimers our flowers. He must have slipped out that side gate. It's dark now. There are so many dangers. He could fall into a well or under the hooves of—''

"Peace, peace, dearling," soothed Thomas. "I have Humfrey alerting every worker on the estate. We'll find him. You bide here with Mistress Mortimer." Then he and the squire hurried outside.

"But of course," the older woman said. Hearing all the excitement, Mistress Mortimer had now joined the group. "Sit down, my dear, and calm yourself," she said. "Why, all my children wandered off at one time or another. You'd never believe where we once found our Jason. He was asleep on—''

"Nay," Rose interrupted, "you stay. I must join the search."

"Oh, God," she prayed as she ran past the stables, "please keep him safe." She could see spots of light fanning out into the darkness as the workers continued their search. "Derry, Derry, where are you?" she cried. "Call out to Mama and I will find you."

"Rose. Over here!" She ran in the direction of Thomas's shout. As she came around the barn she could see Thomas and the squire holding their torches aloft and peering into the wool room, the building which housed the fleeces for later shipment. "Did you find him? Is he safe?" she blurted out as she reached the men. Thomas nodded and put a finger to his lips as he stood aside to let her enter the building. He followed with his torch.

At first she could see nothing but the stacks of newly shorn fleeces. Then, with immense relief, she saw Derry huddled among the fleeces sound asleep. "Thomas, that sound," she whispered. She felt surrounded by a ghostly stirring and sighing.

" 'Tis the fleeces breathing. In the coolness of the night the warmth escapes from them and causes those sounds."

Chapter Three

THAT NIGHT Thomas relented and allowed her to lay Derry between them. As she stroked the little boy's hair, Rose whispered, "Oh, Thomas, if anything happened to Derry, I would not want to go on living."

"Tush, you must not speak so, my dear. Illness takes away so many young children."

"Aye, but I cannot believe God would so miraculously preserve me in prison and allow Derry to be born, and then take him from me."

"We cannot question God's ways."

"Oh, but I have, so many times. Especially after Derick was put to death. I questioned and wondered, and I still wonder why God spared my life when I was set to die at the stake."

"Because you are far too comely to perish in a fire."

"Thomas, I marvel that you can speak so lightly of such horror. Dear young Molly, my cellmate, went to the fires in the bloom of her youth."

"Forgive me, dear. A thoughtless jest by a very sleepy man." He yawned and began to turn to his side but she persisted. "You never saw a burning, did you?"

"Nay, but many a friend and brother in the Lord perished that way. Dr. Taylor from Hadleigh and others I knew."

"You cannot realize what it was like, to share a cell with two fine Christian women and have them taken and not you. The guilt I feel ofttimes overwhelms me."

"But you suffered much in prison."

"Mayhap, but observe me now, in a soft feather bed—"

"I know somewhat of that. Ofttimes while on the Continent I would feel a traitor to be in safety, but then I reasoned that if I had not been able to provide for the young men training for the ministry and enable your brother and others to print tracts against popery, there might not now be as many young ministers grounded in the Word and ready to fill the pulpits of England. I feel I have helped in some small way. And you know I planned to seek out the families of martyrs and aid them."

A chilling thought occurred to Rose. "Thomas, is that why you wed me? As a penance for escaping the flames?"

He sat up and reached across the sleeping child to grasp her hand. "Nay, love, nay. I was drawn to you that first day you arrived in Emden. So comely, so brave a woman to risk your life bringing messages to the exiles and searching for your brother. I had not thought to wed again but you—you captured my heart." He leaned down to kiss her.

"Be careful, you'll awaken Derry."

"The lad's sound asleep. I'll carry him to his own bed. You'll be alone with him soon enough."

"You're returning to London so soon?"

"Nay, I must needs journey to Norwich to see old Basing, my agent to the Norfolk clothiers. He has managed well during my absence on the Continent and has a sound sense of business, but ofttimes he is too staid in his dealing. A visit from me will stir him up to more venturesome commerce. Thence from Norwich, I'll ride to Halifax to promote goodwill among the clothiers there who bring their goods to Blackwell Hall."

"Then shall you return to the manor?"

He shook his head. "Nay, to London to teach Edmund Laxton the ins and outs of shipping and customs. The sooner he learns to act in my stead, the sooner I shall be able to spend more time with you, my whiting."

Rose sat up and rested her chin on her knees. "I just don't understand why you must leave so quickly."

"You didn't marry another blacksmith, dearling," he said gently.

"My work doesn't come to me; I must seek it out. That's why I am called a Merchant Adventurer rather than a mere merchant. Would you rather we owned a shop in London and never budged from it?"

She sighed wistfully. "A little shop in Bury, mayhap, with our rooms in the back—"

"And where would Derry play? In the street?"

"Oh, Thomas, I do love the manor, but you saw how difficult it was for me today. I've never been in charge of a large household before. Could you not at least make a list for me to follow?"

He laughed, "And how should it read? 'Morning: open eyes, get out of bed, go down to breakfast.' Nay, amend that last. 'Dress, then go to breakfast.' Let common sense guide you, dearling. You shall know what to do. The household servants seem worthy of their hire, and Humfrey the overseer shall manage the farm and all matters concerning the tenants. He has charge of the household accounts. If you have need to purchase anything, he will make the funds available. But enough talk." He scooped Derry up in his arms and carried him toward the nursery. "Keep our bed warm, my love, while I take this scamp to his own bed."

The next day when Derry fell asleep in the windowseat in the parlor, Thomas persuaded Rose to leave him in Sybil's care and take a final ride with him before he began packing for his journey to Norwich. They cut across their own fields and soon joined a path which led toward Stowmarket. Rose caught a glimpse of red in the hedgerow which bordered the path and reined in her horse. "Oh, look, Thomas, a briar rose, the first of summer!"

Thomas joined her. "Lovely indeed, my dearling, and further proof that you are well-named." He reached out to pluck it from its thorny branches. "Here, I'll—drat—" A thorn dug into his thumb and he dropped the rose which was promptly trampled under his horse's hooves.

"Never mind, Thomas," she said as she handed him her handkerchief to wipe away the drop of blood, "there'll be other roses."

As they approached a crossroad they could see a black dog furiously digging in the center of the road. Thomas spurred his horse ahead and chased the mongrel away from the hole it had made. He had dismounted and was peering into the excavation when Rose caught up with him. "What is it?" she asked. "What was the dog after?"

Thomas took hold of her horse's bridle. "Don't look," he warned, but it was too late. Rose was staring down into the face of a corpse. Although still partially covered with dirt, she could tell it was the face of a young woman. She screamed and her horse began to shy away, but Thomas kept a firm hand on the bridle and led the animal a few yards away and then helped Rose dismount. She buried her face in Thomas's shoulder. "That horrid dog," she murmured, "did it—is she—?"

"Nay, it hadn't yet touched her flesh. She must have been buried during the night," he continued grimly. "If they must bury criminals and witches in the crossroads, they could at least do it decently and dig a deep grave."

"She didn't look like a criminal. She might have taken her life because of some inward grief. They bury suicides in such a manner also. Poor thing." Rose began to weep softly.

"Well, whatever the cause, you rest by the hedgerow and I'll cover her up again."

In spite of herself, Rose watched as Thomas began scooping the loose dirt into the shallow grave. Then his hand paused and he began brushing away the dirt again. "I've found the reason for her burial here. There is a wooden stake driven into her heart. She must have been a witch."

"Thomas, let her be, let her be," Rose cried out and began leading her mount back toward the manor.

"Ride on ahead," Thomas said. "I'll cover up the grave and place some stones upon it to keep that dog from returning and then I will catch up with you."

Rose passed the spot in the hedgerow where the flower had bloomed and she glanced down at the crushed petals on the ground. When Thomas caught up with her she asked, "Do you suppose she was truly a witch? She had such a fair countenance."

"Even Satan himself is disguised as an angel of light. Besides, we did not behold her when she was still alive."

"But she was so young. If she were a witch, then some evil beldame must have led her astray."

"Yea, superstitious folk abound in these parts. And 'tis odd—

the same villagers that bury a dead sheep in the gateway to prevent the rest of their flock from falling ill will be the first to accuse their neighbors of sorcery. Only the light of Christ's truth can drive away such darkness of superstition."

"That poor girl might never have heard the gospel proclaimed."

"Or she might have heard and rejected it. There are those that deliberately choose to worship Satan and they must be stopped."

"But, Thomas!" protested Rose, "to kill someone and drive a stake through her heart—is that the way to stop evil? Did not our Lord say, 'Love your enemies?' "

"Ah, Rose, you have a woman's tender heart. Let's speak of pleasanter things."

But Rose couldn't stop thinking about the dead woman. *Had she been abused and mocked by an angry mob? No doubt,* she thought. *And I can just see the expressions on their faces. The same expressions I saw through the bars of the cage on London Bridge.* For Rose had been publicly displayed in a cage as a heretic. She knew that the very Londoners who had spat upon her and reviled her then might well have been the same onlookers who doffed their caps and curtsied as she walked by in her wedding procession a few weeks ago. How fickle were men's hearts. Hadn't it always been so? The same crowd which joyously greeted the Lord as He entered Jerusalem mocked Him as He carried His cross to Calvary.

She sighed. *I thought I was truly beginning a new life when I married Thomas, leaving all the memories of sorrow and suffering behind, but there is no escaping tragedy in this wicked world. Whether that girl was a witch or not, evil was behind her death, and the devil must laugh because he has captured another soul. Aye, he is our true foe, for the Scripture says, "We wrestle not against flesh and blood, but against principalities, against powers, against the rulers of the darkness of this world, against spiritual wickedness in high places." Be on guard, my girl,* she told herself. *You thought you had fought the fight and could lay your armor down and be at ease, but 'tis not so. Be on your guard.*

Chapter Four

AT DAWN THE next morning Thomas set off for Norwich. Rose waved to him from the bedchamber window as he rode out of the courtyard and then she lay back on the featherbed and snuggled her head into the silken pillow. *Rose Stratton, lady of the manor*, she thought dreamily and then drifted back to sleep.

She dreamed she was Queen Elizabeth. She was dressed in a scarlet gown of velvet and a cape made of gold cloth. She was riding a milk white stallion through the streets of London. Hundreds of people lined the streets and bowed as she passed. She was pleased to see that all of the onlookers were also finely dressed, with not a ragged beggar or sickly child among them. All the children had rosy cheeks and sturdy limbs and were carried on the shoulders of their handsome fathers.

On she rode down the surprisingly immaculate street of Cheapside until she passed through Newgate and entered Smithfield. A golden glow in the field almost blinded her. Someone handed her a silver bucket filled with water and a bejeweled ladle. Slowly she rode toward the glow until she could see a hundred stakes with a martyr tied to each one. Flames were licking at their feet and their faces were contorted with pain. Slowly she rode to each one and dipped out a few drops of water onto their heads. "More water!" she cried out, "I must have more—"

She was awakened by a loud knock on the door. "Enter!" she cried out. The pinched face of the little chambermaid peeked shyly around the door.

"Pardon, Mistress, 'tis Master Humfrey begging a word with you downstairs. A most urgent problem, he says."

Rose jumped out of bed and quickly dressed as the young chambermaid smoothed the bedcovers. "What is it, girl?" Rose asked. "A fire, an injury to one of the farm workers?" She nervously coiled her hair into a bun and thought with dismay how little she knew about treating burns or broken bones.

" 'Tis hogs, madam."

"Hogs?"

"Aye, madam. Master Humfrey says you must do something about the hogs."

"Oh, dear Lord, help me," she prayed as she slipped on her shoes. *What if a great boar has seriously injured a farmhand?* She glanced over the gallery railing as she hurried toward the stairs. The overseer was standing just inside the great hall by the linenfold screen. A tall man and in his fifties, he seemed much younger except for a slight stoop to his shoulders and his iron-gray hair. Unlike other outdoor workers, he didn't seem ill at ease in his master's house as he chatted with the cook and Sybil, the housemaid. Rose saw that Tad, the stableboy, was with him, peering in awe at the large tapestry hanging on the wall, which illustrated the story of Jonah and the great fish. All the servants turned to watch Rose descend the stairs.

"Good day, Humfrey, what trouble brings you here so early?" she asked in a slightly quavering voice.

The overseer nodded a greeting and then looked away as if he were studying a far pasture. At length he replied, "Three of our hogs be mortally ill, madam." He spoke slowly and deliberately, jutting out his full lower lip for emphasis.

"But surely the swineherd—" she began.

He plowed right on, "Them hogs, a boar and two sows, has their throats so swollen up from eating wet grain. Look like bullfrogs, they do. Hog bullfrogs, they be." Humfrey chuckled at his own joke and the other servants joined in and then grew quiet as they waited for her next words.

They're testing me, she realized. "What do you suggest we do, Humfrey?" *Good girl*, she told herself. *Throw it back to him.*

Humfrey folded his hands across his chest. "There's owt to do save watch 'em die unless—'' He paused and looked off again.

"Unless?"

"Unless I cut on 'em.'' He swung his hand across his own throat. "Slit the swollen mass and let the putrid liquid out.''

Rose felt a wave of nausea and took hold of the bannister to steady herself. *Fine conversation before I've broken my fast*, she thought. "Cut on them then,'' she ordered weakly.

"Could do, but my last master forbade it when his best breeder swolled up.''

"And what happened to the beast?'' Talking to Humfrey was like walking through a maze, she was learning. She might never find the exit, but one minute longer and she would end the discussion by retching in front of the servants.

"Died, it did,'' he said finally.

"Then I give you permission to cut—to relieve the poor beasts' swelling. Now, Bess, will you lay out mine and Derry's breakfast? I'll go and awaken him.'' Humfrey lumbered out and Bess scurried into the kitchen, but Tad, Mary and Sybil lingered. Rose pointed a finger at the stableboy. "You, my lad, don't you have cows to groom? The servants laughed and then Rose caught her error. She was in too bad a mood by then to laugh at her own slip of the tongue and she glared at the three servants.

"Look you, I am not quite the idiot my speech betrays. I was raised on a farm and wed to a blacksmith. I well know the difference between a cow and a horse. 'Tis just that I am unused to being in charge of so large a dwelling but since''—she raised her voice and put her hands on her hips—"*but since I am the mistress of this manor, I will take charge.*'' She fixed her eyes on the stableboy until all traces of an insolent grin disappeared from his face. "Tad, you shall stay in the kitchen and help cook all day. I'm certain Bess has many pots for you to scrub. Sybil and Mary, you know your duties. Get to them.''

As Rose climbed the stairs she heard Sybil tell Mary in a loud whisper, "I marvel she didn't tell Tad to milk the horses.''

For the next few weeks Rose was kept busy settling daily disputes between Sybil and Bess, and comforting Mary, the little chambermaid whom Sybil had in tears most of the time. Humfrey continued to bring her the most minor problems to solve, and she would dump them back into his lap.

One afternoon as Rose returned from the market at Bury, Sybil handed her a letter, saying, "A messenger brought it. Nosey body he is. Asked questions about you and Master Derry. I shooed him off. He's at the stables waiting for your reply."

Rose thought it must be from Thomas, so she carried it up to her bedchamber to read it privately. It was from Joan. In bold, large strokes she had skipped a salutation and plunged in with:

> Well, Rose, have you not had your fill of country life by now? I've instructed my messenger to report all he sees and I well expect him to describe you as having your gown adorned with chicken feathers and your shoes with manure. You no doubt are spending your time fleeing from angry boars and nipping geese while Derry watches and laughs.
>
> I do miss the sound of the lad's laughter. I miss you both.
>
> London is the same. The plague seems to be passing us by this summer. I've received a new shipment of lace that is so fine it rivals butterfly wings. Come down to see your old friend and we shall make you a gown that all the ladies of the court will envy. They will look like mud-hens beside you. Although where you would wear such finery in Suffolk wilds, I know not. Perhaps to a calving or a hog butchering.
>
> Kiss Derry for me.
>
> Joan

Rose smiled and took out a sheet of foolscap to reply.

Dear Joan,

> I do miss you, dear friend. Thomas is away at the moment and I have no one to converse with apart from hearing the servants' endless disputes. I would even enjoy one of our arguments about religion.
>
> Derry still asks why Aunty Joan isn't with us, and whenever I scold him, he wails loudly for you.
>
> I am joyed to hear the plague hasn't arisen this year, but there are still evil humors in the crowded city and I dare not travel with Derry just yet. We would always welcome a visit from you.
>
> I know not how your messenger will describe my appearance, but 'tis easier to keep my shoes clean here on the manor than it was walking about in the muck of London's streets. Come and see for yourself.
>
> Love from Rose and Derry

As Rose watched Joan's messenger ride off with her reply, a feeling of loneliness settled about her like a heavy woolen shawl.

Mayhap I should have resided in Thomas's townhouse for a season after our wedding. But he was so pleased he had purchased the manor. Still, if I had known Thomas would leave me here alone— How can we build a strong marriage if we are together so little? She turned and almost tripped over a bucket someone had left by the steps.

With a scowl she kicked the empty bucket and sent it rolling across the courtyard. A startled hen hopped out of its way and began clucking a reproach.

"Chicken feathers!" Rose muttered and flounced inside.

As lady of the manor, she soon learned she was expected to be physician and surgeon to farm workers and tenants alike. She was inadequate to the task because she had never learned the skills of doctoring. There was always her aunt or some other woman in her village of Boxton who knew the herbs and droughts to prescribe. A grisly incident soon relieved her of that responsibility: When Humfrey brought an injured mower to her and she saw his left thumb dangling by a thread of flesh, she fainted dead away. Thereafter the cook assumed her role as physician.

A messenger brought a letter from Thomas which begged her forgiveness for his prolonged absence. "Business matters" was all the reason he gave, but the rest of the letter was filled with romantic phrases which told of his longing for her. She blushed to read them. She couldn't sleep that night and the next morning took Derry out for a stroll around the farm.

The little boy was fascinated by the chickenhouse and began doing an imitation of a hen scratching and clucking. He held his arms akimbo and turned his head just as a hen does when she pecks and listens, pecks and listens. "Well done, my lad," Rose praised him and clapped her hands. "Truly you have a gift for mime." At last he tired of imitating the chickens and she led him quickly around the pigsty and past the toolshed.

"Them hoes be dull, sir," a young worker was saying to Humfrey. "By your leave, I could take 'em over to the smith's."

"Nay, lad," she heard Humfrey reply. "Just give 'em to old Morris to grind on our stone."

The youth went dejectedly toward the carpenter shop and the overseer spotted Rose. He gestured toward the youth. "The workers, they'd go t' smithy for any little reason just to get a bit of gossip."

Rose nodded and walked on with Derry, remembering Derick's smithy by their cottage in Boxton. She recalled the sight of him with his strong back bent over the anvil, his muscular arm raising the hammer. She could almost feel the vibration of the clanging steel. She could see his coal-black hair curling on his neck. The feel of her lips on that neck, the smell of iron on his skin—she started and looked around guiltily. Derick was gone. She mustn't think of him that way anymore. She was wed to another. She put her hands on her burning cheeks and tried to think of Thomas. How strange that now after Thomas had reawakened the physical expression of love in her, she could only see Derick's face and remember his touch. But after all, how many nights had she lain in Derick's arms? *Thomas, think of Thomas,* she told herself. *He will be home soon and we will grow even closer in heart and mind.*

But that night she dreamt of Derick, not Thomas. The next morning she arose before Derry and, weary of eating alone, took her plate into the kitchen. Bess was kneading dough and seemed flustered that Rose should sit at the table. Rose tried to start a conversation. "Were you born in Goodthorpe, Bess?"

"Nay. Bury," the cook replied and pummeled the dough.

"Do you have a husband?"

"Did."

"Oh, I was widowed also. My husband died as a martyr."

The cook looked at her with new interest. "I have a friend—a martyr's widow, who lives on the road to Bury. She's in sore distress. Malorie's her name. She has a cottage full of children and tries to survive by knitting. Her eldest son used to hire out to farms, but he died of poisoned blood last harvest time."

Rose recovered from the shock of hearing such a long speech from the taciturn woman. "What a tragedy. We must do something to help her."

The cook wiped her forehead, leaving a flour streak across it. "I was wondering, might I take my friend some scraps of food now and then? I'd take nothing costly; just some coarse bread or a bit of cheese."

Rose felt a stab of guilt. She had been needy and dependent upon others for so long. Yet she hadn't thought of personally ministering to the poor now that she had plenty. "Of course we shall help feed them," she told Bess. "Why don't you gather up a large basket of food, and I'll take them to her myself. Just tell me how to find her cottage."

Rose went upstairs, awakened and dressed Derry, then changed her own clothes for riding. After giving Derry his breakfast they were on their way to the stables when she met Humfrey and two men in the courtyard.

"Good day, madam," Humfrey said. "These be the workmen the master desired me to hire." The two men bowed. "They'll be working on the hearth in the great hall, enlarging it as the master ordered. I've cautioned them not to leave a mess or scratch the floors."

"Very well—oh—and Humfrey, I desire to speak with you privately." She waited while the overseer motioned for the men to wait by their cart. After walking a few steps toward the house, she began, "I've just heard of a family in dire straits, and I shall need about twenty shillings to aid them."

He rubbed his jaw. " 'Tis a large sum to give away."

She lifted her chin and glared up at him. "What is that to you? It is not your money."

"Nay, it is not, madam, but the master set me as a steward over it."

Her eyes welled up with angry tears, and she refused to brush them away. "Did Master Stratton not order you to see to my needs?" she almost shouted.

"Aye, madam. Yours, but not those of slothful cottagers."

"Enough!" She grabbed Derry's hand with such force that she almost threw him off balance as she marched toward the stables. Then she swung around and ordered, "Humfrey, I desire funds to purchase cloth for a new gown."

He looked at her for a moment and then bowed. "Certainly, madam. How much do you need?"

It was her turn to pause and rub her chin. "Let me consider—I shall have it faced with damask, with sleeves of satin—oh, I think twenty shillings shall do nicely."

Rose carried Derry on her horse and brought Tad along on an old mare to carry the basket of food and some blankets. Although the days were quite warm, she well knew how cold and damp a cottage could become after a summer rain. She found Widow Malorie's cottage quite easily. It appeared the entire family was out in the garden. As they rode up she saw three little boys of stairstep heights digging in the barren ground. Two older girls sat beside their mother on a bench under a large oak tree. All three of them were busily knitting. A little girl about Derry's age was playing with a scrap of yarn and a stick. "Widow Malorie?" The woman nodded and stood up.

"Good day to you. I'm Rose Stratton," she said, lifting Derry off after her and holding him tight. "Your friend Bess is my cook."

The widow smiled and walked over to open the gate. She had a pleasant smile but as she approached, Rose could see her face was etched with many fine wrinkles, noting great suffering. Her jaw and neck had the sagging skin of a plump person who had recently lost much weight. "Good day to you, madam," she motioned for Rose to enter the garden. She looked puzzled and Rose could tell she was trying not to look at the basket of food Tad carried. The boys and the little girl came to see what was happening, but the two older girls hung back.

"Here, Tad," Rose called, setting Derry down. "Hand the basket to me and then find some water for the horses." Rose held out the basket to the widow. "I'd be pleased if you'd accept this gift from my husband and me." One of the boys stood on tiptoe to look into the basket Rose held out.

"Mama, there's bread and cheese and—"

"Hush, William. Go inside," his mother ordered. "Thank you, madam, but I cannot accept charity. The Lord will meet our needs." The widow looked down in embarrassment.

Rose put her hand on the woman's shoulder. "But can you not see, dear sister, this is how He is meeting your needs today. I am so grateful God has given me the means to help you."

The widow's face brightened. "Oh, then you are a believer too?"

Tears spilled down Rose's face. "My dear, I too was widowed when my first husband was burned at the stake. Now please, accept this food in Jesus' name."

The other woman wiped her eyes with her apron. "Oh, I shall, with gratefulness. 'Tis just that ever since my John died, there has been no one who truly understands. Bess is kind, but she thinks my husband lost his wits when he stood firm in his faith."

"Mama, can we have some of the bread?" asked the smallest boy.

"Of course! Anne—Jane," she called. The oldest girl came up followed by her younger sister. "Greet this fine lady. She knows our Lord. This is Anne, my eldest daughter, and Jane." They curtsied. Rose was struck by the oldest girl's delicate beauty. She had pale, almost white hair and a heart-shaped face. "Take the food into the house and feed all the children," Widow Malorie said, handing the basket to Anne who went inside, followed by the rest of the children, including Derry.

The widow led Rose to the bench under the oak. "Do sit down and forgive me for my burst of self-pity. The Lord is faithful. I just miss John and my oldest son, Richard, he—"

"I know," Rose said softly. "Bess told me what befell your son." They both sat silent for a few moments. Then Rose said, "Let us speak of the future. You must allow me to send provisions over regularly."

"Oh, but I can work to earn our food if I just had enough yarn to make garments to sell at markets and fairs."

Rose emptied her purse of the coins she had extracted from Humfrey. "Is this enough for a start?" she asked.

"Oh, more than enough, but I couldn't—"

"Nonsense," Rose interrupted. "My husband is a Merchant Adventurer. I shall go into business also. I'll seek out other widows who can knit. Then I'll buy their supplies and market them." After discussing their plans Rose began to tell her how she was caught with messages from the exiles, about Newgate Prison, and how she accepted Christ as her Savior there in her cell. She even told Widow Malorie how she was spared execution by an error in the warrant and how Joan managed to spirit Derry away to safety after he was born in prison.

"Upon my word, Mistress Stratton, you have endured much!"

"Please call me Rose. I'm sorry I talked at length about myself, Widow Malorie."

"Please call me Margaret. Oh no, my dear, 'tis good to talk. Tell me, Rose, have you ever entertained doubts?"

"About my salvation?"

"Nay, I meant about what the deaths of all the martyrs accomplished. It discourages me so. Aside from the end of popery, there doesn't seem to be many real changes in the churches. You haven't attended church in Goodthorpe, have you?"

"Nay, we've only held our own worship service in our chapel, and with Thomas gone I have been neglecting that, I'm afraid. Thomas says that the minister in Goodthorpe might as well officiate in Rome. You and your family must worship with us."

"The lord and lady of the manor may well get by without attending the parish church, but the likes of me would still be punished if I did not attend. As you say, the service is little changed from the time my dear John refused to attend Mass."

"Thomas says the Queen feels she must move slowly. In the meantime there are so many ministers conducting services in so many ways, he says we will not be noticed if we go our own way and follow Christ as we feel the Scriptures lead us."

Just then Anne emerged from the cottage carrying Derry. Like the other children who trailed after, he had blue stains all around his mouth. *Bess must have packed some blackberry tarts*, thought Rose.

"Anne, clean that child's face," said Margaret.

"Never you mind," Rose told the girl. "I'll do it. Hand my scalawag over." She reached out for Derry but he drew back.

"Play Anne," he said. "Ride horsey." Anne put him up on her shoulders and skipped over to where Tad had tethered the two horses. Derry was laughing with delight.

"He's surely taken with Anne," commented Rose, a little jealous.

"Ah, all the children love Anne. She has a gentle but firm way with them and can make even her brothers tow the mark." The widow sighed. "We shall all miss her."

"Where is she going?"

"To London, come August. I have a niece who's in service to a wealthy family. They've agreed to take Anne on as a scullery maid."

The thought of that frail child toiling in a kitchen in the steaming London heat appalled Rose. She thought of a way to spare her, but would have to ask Thomas first. She stood up to go. "Farewell, Margaret. You must come to Grendal Hall for a visit."

"Oh, I couldn't do that. Bess tells me what a grand place it is. Nay, I'll be at my knitting and trying to seek out other Christian families in need as you've asked me."

"Well, I'll return to visit you, if I may. Your fellowship has done me good."

The stoneworkers' cart was still in the courtyard when Rose arrived at Grendal Hall. When she entered she saw the two workers watching as Sybil knelt down and was placing something under a hearthstone.

"Whatever are you doing?" Rose demanded. "Show me that object."

Sybil stood up slowly and then showed her a heart-shaped bit of red cloth pierced all through with pins.

"A charm? Who gave you leave to place a witch charm in my house?"

" 'Tis common practice in these parts, madam, to place such a charm beneath the hearthstone to turn away any evil spell that might be cast on they that dwell in the house." Sybil spoke slowly and clearly as if she were teaching a child.

"Give me that." Rose snatched the charm from Sybil's open hand and hurried to the kitchen, still carrying Derry. Sybil followed and entered just in time to see Rose casting the charm into the coals in the large hearth. "There. We will have no charms or other witchery in this house. Is that clear? We will trust in the Lord." Derry had begun to cry at the sound of her raised voice.

"Yea, madam," replied Sybil softly, with no sign of emotion on her face. She held her arms out. "I'll just take little Master Derry for his nap."

Rose pulled away. "Nay, I'll do it myself."

"But I always—" Sybil had grown used to helping with Derry, relegating the housework to Mary.

"You have other work to do today," said Rose, trying to calm down. "Go out and scrape the dovecote."

"The dovecote?" Sybil's eyes widened. " 'Tis a task for the stableboy."

" 'Tis your task if I make it so. Now go." Rose's heart was beating fast as Sybil stared in disbelief, her face white and her lips pressed in a tight line. Rose felt that she would back down in a moment, so she turned away from Sybil and said, "Clean it, I say." The maid must be taught a lesson.

Sybil went out without another word, and Rose took Derry upstairs and lay down with him on her own bed. *To think if I had not come in, that wicked charm would be under our very hearthstone. I wish Thomas were here. Was I too harsh? That poor girl knows no better. I must instruct her. Still, a witch's charm! Cottage or manor house, there will be no witchcraft in my home. Ever!*

Chapter Five

THE NEXT MORNING Rose announced to the household that she would hold a Bible study that evening which they would all be required to attend. As she searched the Scriptures for the right text, she found these commands in Deuteronomy 18:10-12: "There shall not be found among you any one that maketh his son or his daughter to pass through the fire, or that useth divination, or an observer of times, or an enchanter, or a witch, or a charmer, or a consulter with familiar spirits, or a wizard, or a necromancer. For all that do these things are an abomination unto the Lord: and because of these abominations the Lord thy God doth drive them out from before thee."

She also marked Galatians 5:19-21 to read to them. "Now the works of the flesh are manifest, which are these; adultery, fornication, uncleanness, lasciviousness, idolatry, witchcraft, hatred, variance, emulations, wrath, strife, seditions, heresies, envyings, murders, drunkenness, revellings, and such like: of the which I tell you before, as I have also told you in time past, that they which do such things shall not inherit the kingdom of God."

There, that ought to be plain enough for them to understand, she thought. *'Tis not their fault that they cling to superstition. They've not been taught the truth.* She remembered how Elinore, one of the other Christian women who had been imprisoned with her at Newgate, had taught her the Scriptures from a Bible she had smuggled in under her clothing. Dear Elinore—her twisted, crippled body was whole now in heaven.

That afternoon Rose took Derry for a short horseback ride to soothe him for his naptime. On the way back she noticed Tad leading a beautiful black stallion into the stable. *Thomas is home,* she thought happily, *and he's purchased a new mount.* As she approached the porch, she beckoned to the gardener's boy to lift Derry down so she could dismount. With the sleepy child in her arms, carefully watching her feet so as not to trip on the stone steps, Rose bumped into someone standing in her way. Startled, she stumbled backward.

"Oh, pardon—why, Edmund Laxton—what are you—Thomas, has something happened to Thomas?"

"Nay, calm yourself," he laughed, amused at her distress. "Thomas had to abide in London a few more days, but he was anxious for your welfare and I offered to ride up ahead. It will give us time to get better acquainted."

In the muggy July heat, Edmund had removed his doublet. His linen shirt hung open to the waist, revealing his broad chest—glistening with perspiration in the hot sun.

"Here, let me help you with the lad." As Edmund attempted to take Derry from her, the frightened child threw his arms around Rose's neck, causing the young man to lose his balance. Or so it first seemed to Rose. But when he leaned against her longer then was necessary, she firmly pushed him away.

"I'll carry my son inside," she snapped, struggling to regain her composure. Edmund relinquished his hold on the boy but continued to gaze down at her. Rose blushed as she self-consciously began tucking her wind-blown hair into her bonnet. *I must look a fright,* she thought, *but why should it bother me? What is it about this man that flusters me so?* She hurried inside. "Sybil! Sybil!" she called and was embarrassed to find the maid just inside the entrance way. "Oh, there you are. Some cider for our guest and tell the cook to lay an extra place for supper. And tell Mary to prepare the south chamber for Master Laxton." She would be civil to the young man for Thomas's sake, but she would bed him as far away from her own chamber as possible.

"Lovely gown," Edmund said at supper. "It matches your eyes." Rose looked down at her plate and scolded herself for changing into her blue silk.

"My eyes are more green than blue," she protested, nervously crumbling a piece of bread.

"Let me see for myself." He stood up and leaned across the table.

"Master Laxton! Have a care—the candles—you'll catch fire!"

"Blue. As blue as the Bay of Naples." He smiled broadly and settled back into his chair. Sybil came in with a tray and began serving. "Well, well, oysters in gravy. Madam, you dine me royally."

" 'Tis nothing," said Rose. "I had ordered oysters to be sent from the coast as soon as St. James's day was past. I had thought Thomas would have returned and—"

"And we all know what oysters do to a man, don't we?" Edmund grinned. While Rose blushed, Sybil gave him a knowing look and brushed against him as she served him another oyster.

They ate in silence for a while, but his continual staring made Rose uncomfortable. She decided conversation would be more bearable. "You mentioned Italy, Edmund. Have you traveled much?"

"Not enough. Wanderlust is one thing I have in common with Thomas, although why he would care to leave such a fair bride, I cannot know."

"He only travels on business," declared Rose in her husband's defense.

"Ah, but I've heard him talk of longing to see faraway lands. 'Tis one of his sorrows that he could not make the journey to Muscovy with Willoughby."

"But I heard that only one ship of three survived that journey and Willoughby himself perished before he reached that land. Such adventuring is fraught with danger."

"Aye, but some men love danger and love sailing close to the wind." He reached out and caught her hand just as Sybil returned to clear away the dishes.

Rose pulled her hand out of his grasp and stood up. "Well, good night, Master Laxton. I must go up and see about Derry and then retire."

"But, Mistress," Sybil said coyly, "were you not going to teach us the Scriptures tonight?"

"Aye, but since we have a houseguest who doesn't—who wouldn't—"

Edmund held up his hand, "Please, dear lady, don't let me deter you from your Christian duty.'' He smiled and lounged back in Thomas's carved chair.

Rose lifted her chin and then sat back down. The young buck was not going to embarrass her anymore. "Very well, Sybil, fetch the Bible from my bedchamber. I expect the Word of God will do Master Laxton and all of us great good.''

When the servants were all seated about the table, she drew a candlestick nearer and found the verses in Deuteronomy and read them aloud. Then she turned to the verses in Galatians and with a louder voice read the list of fleshly works with great emphasis—adultery, fornication, and so on—to the end.

" 'Pon my word, you are quite the hot gospeller,'' said Edmund with a look of mock surprise. "Now please interpret those verses to our weak and worldly minds.'' He glanced at the servants and was rewarded with a smirk and a nod from Sybil.

Rose cleared her throat and reached for her mug of cider. After a quick sip she said, "I think I shall let the Scriptures speak for themselves, except to say that there will be no witchcraft nor for— nor any other fleshly sins mentioned performed under my roof. Now I must tuck Derry in. Bess,'' she told the middle-aged cook, "you conduct Master Laxton to his chamber. Good night to you.''

"But surely you'll return, Mistress Stratton,'' said Edmund in formal tones. "I am not a child that I would retire this early and 'twould be discourteous of you to leave a houseguest to sit by the parlor fire alone.''

She hesitated. After all, he was Thomas's assistant and her guest. "Very well, I will come down a little later.'' She led Derry upstairs and deliberately took her time telling him bedtime stories and stroking his hair until he fell asleep. When she returned to the parlor, Edmund was sitting in Thomas's large chair by the fire and had moved her smaller chair next to his. She moved it a few feet away from his and sat down.

"I took the liberty of telling the servants they could retire,'' he said nonchalantly.

"That was very—considerate of you,'' Rose murmured. She would force herself to have a few minutes of civil conversation with the young hotspur and then retire and bolt her bedchamber door.

"I shall now regale you with tales of my travels in Italy," Edmund boasted.

"One tale, and then to bed." She spoke firmly, as to a child.

He began with a hilarious account of his arrival in Florence. Rose began laughing in spite of herself. He did have a flair for storytelling and soon she could picture the green hills above Rome and red-tiled houses of Florence. As the last log on the fire dogs broke and crumbled into the ashes, she suddenly realized they had been sitting there for hours.

"Oh, I must retire!" she cried, jumping up in the middle of one of his stories.

He merely smiled and followed her closely as she extinguished the tapers on the mantle. Reaching for the last flickering candle on a cupboard she said, "I shall light the way to your chamber."

"Most gracious of you, madam," he said, giving her an elaborate bow.

He followed her up the stairs and along the gallery to the south chamber. She stood back from the door to his chamber and said, "Good night. May you rest well."

He leaned his hand on the lintel of the doorway just as Derick used to do in their cottage. He towered over her, his unruly black locks falling over his forehead. Touching her arm he whispered softly, "Will you not also light the way to my bed?" So much did he remind her of Derick at that moment that as he bent his face toward hers, she almost lifted her lips to meet his. She caught herself just in time and stepped suddenly backward, spilling the hot wax from her candle onto Edmund's hand. He cursed loudly and then laughed as she ran toward her own bedchamber, slamming and bolting the door.

She collapsed against the door and tried to catch her breath. The sound of her own heartbeat pounded in her ears. "Flee immorality, flee immorality." The Bible verse ran through her head. "Oh, thank you, Father," she prayed, "thank you for helping me to flee just in time. How could I have almost yielded to a kiss from another man?" For an instant, in her loneliness she had allowed Edmund's image to merge with the memory of her beloved first husband, but never again, she told herself. Edmund's cruel laughter would ring in her ears each time she saw him. She would deliberately bring it to mind. Rose fell asleep praying that Thomas would return soon.

She avoided Edmund the next morning by taking breakfast in her room and then slipping into the kitchen while he was out for a walk. Toward noon, however, he found her in the kitchen busily shelling peas while Derry played under the kitchen table. "There you are," he said. "Hiding in the kitchen of all places. Aren't you going to show me about the manor?"

"Nay, I cannot," she answered curtly. "I must help the cook prepare for dinner."

"But, madam, I can easily—" Bess began to protest. But she fell silent when Rose gave her a sharp look.

Edmund sat down on the bench beside Rose and began shelling peas. He followed her all day, but she managed to see that they were never alone together. When Thomas rode into the courtyard late in the afternoon, he had barely dismounted before Rose fairly flew into his arms.

"Oh, Thomas, I've missed you so!" she cried, and kissed him. Edmund looked on with an amused expression and Thomas patted her awkwardly on the back. "I've missed you, too, dear."

The talk at supper was all of business. Edmund looked attentive as Thomas discussed the pros and cons of acquiring codfishing rights in Newfoundland waters and of the fluctuation in the price of broad-cloths, and bemoaned the exorbitant rates of custom duty. By now Rose could tell when the young man was playacting. She was an interested listener, but when she interrupted Thomas several times with questions, he grew impatient with her. "Now, my whiting, why trouble your head with business terms? I fear we men have bored you with our talk."

"Nay, Thomas, I was just wondering how—"

But he turned to Edmund and was saying, "I fear I must quit the silk trade. There's too much travel back and forth to the Antwerp Mart. I should sail to the Continent in a few days, but I do wish to survey the manor and oversee the corn harvest."

"Joan taught me that silk—" Rose began, but was interrupted by Edmund this time. "But, sir," he was saying, " 'tis such a profitable market. Surely you could teach me to be your agent in Antwerp. The officials there must remember my father's good name, and I have no family ties to keep me in England."

Thomas thought for a moment. "You do make a good argument, Edmund. If you agree to carefully follow all my instructions, I shall let you be my agent in Antwerp. Will that please you, Rose?"

"Indeed it will," she replied. To think of having Thomas home for a while and Edmund safely across the North Sea pleased her very much. While the two men made plans, she excused herself and went upstairs to kiss Derry good night. She had allowed Sybil to give him supper in the nursery. *I'll speak kindly to her*, she thought. *She does take good care of Derry.*

The door to the nursery was slightly open and she heard Sybil's voice saying, "Then the miller circled the mere three times and called up the devil and he dragged the screaming children down into the fathomless pit—"

Rose burst into the room. "I have warned you. Now you must leave my house! How dare you frighten my child with your witch stories!"

Sybil stood up and faced her calmly. " 'Tis but a fairy tale that every child in these parts knows by heart. The lad is not frightened, are you, Derry?"

Derry was sitting up in his bed, clutching his coverlet. Only his wide brown eyes were showing above it as he shook his head. "Nay," he said breathlessly. But the knuckles of his hands were white.

Rose pointed to the door. "Go to your chamber, Sybil. I will not abide disobedience. You are dismissed from my service."

Sybil took a step closer and said in slow, deliberate tones, "The day I am dismissed I shall tell the master what you and handsome Master Laxton were doing last night after you had hustled us all to our beds."

"What?—I did nothing wrong," Rose stammered, but she felt her face burning.

"Mayhap you did and mayhap you did not, but when I tell my tale to Master Stratton, he might never believe for a certainty that you were not unfaithful to him. And from what I observe of Laxton, that young buck would say nothing to verify your chastity if it cast a stone at his vanity."

She's right, Rose thought. *Even if Thomas wanted to believe me, he might always wonder. We are so newly wed and his harboring doubts might always cause a rift between us. And he so reveres the memory of Edmund's father that he would be loath to accuse Edmund of any unwelcomed advances.* "You are not dismissed from our employ," she said weakly. "Just go to your chamber." Sybil curtsied with a smirk on her face and left the room. Rose paced the floor, carrying Derry until he fell asleep and she calmed down.

Later, alone in their bedchamber, Thomas embraced her but she didn't respond to his kiss. "What's wrong, Rose? You seemed so joyed to see me this afternoon. What troubles you, my whiting?"

She took a deep breath. " 'Tis the maidservant, Sybil. She—". She floundered for words but dare not tell him, she decided, not yet. "She's not a suitable nurse for Derry," she finished lamely.

"Dismiss her then," he said and kissed her forehead. "You know better than I about servant matters."

She pulled away from him, "Nay, I won't do that, but I would like to hire a nurse."

"Whatever you wish," he murmured, kissing her neck.

"I know just the girl—the daughter of a martyr and she—"

His kiss stopped her in midsentence. She relaxed and kissed him back. Anne, a good Christian girl, would be Derry's nurse. With Edmund leaving and Sybil no longer attending Derry, her problems were solved. Or so she thought as she allowed Thomas to lead her to their bed.

Chapter Six

THE SWEET, MUSTY scent of the wheatfields wafted in on an early morning breeze. Rose opened her eyes and stretched. Thomas was already dressed and seated under the shaft of sunlight which streamed in from the open windeye. An open Bible was on his lap and his lips moved silently as he read the Scriptures. His lean, handsome face was set in an expression of deep concentration. Although not as muscular as one who did much physical labor, he had a quiet strength about him. Watching him, Rose thanked God again for giving her a Christian gentleman to wed. *He is my provider and lover*, she thought, *but will we ever become truly one and share our thoughts and dreams?* Perhaps that was too much to hope for. After all, even though she and Derick had loved each other with all the passion of first love, she had not been able to share his joy in receiving Christ. It had been months after his death, when she too had come to believe, that she could finally understand his feelings. *At least Thomas and I share a common faith*, she thought. But watching him read reminded her of how little time she had spent of late in study and communion with God.

"Good morning, dear. Did I awaken you?"

"Nay, Thomas, pray go on with your reading." She arose and began to dress.

"I completed the passage. I was reading in Galatians where you had marked the spot. Edmund told me how you instructed the servants on the night of his arrival. Have you been conducting a weekly Bible

51

study as well as the Sabbath chapel service? I am proud of you for it."

"Of a truth, that was the first time I read the Scriptures to them." Her voice was muffled as she slipped her gown over her head, her back to Thomas.

"But at least on the Sabbath—"

"Nay," she said softly, feeling miserable.

"Tush, madam, you must lead our servants in the way."

His formal expression and the chastening tone of his voice incensed Rose, and she whirled around to face him. "Lead our servants, *sir*," she rejoined. "Lead them? Do you understand all that 'leading our servants' entails? While you are absent I must supervise the household work and settle the servants' squabbles, besides hear every minor problem with man or beast of the farm."

"But surely Humfrey attends—"

"Humfrey, your wise and effectual overseer, delights in heaping his burdens on my shoulders. And he jealously guards the household moneys so that I must outwit him if I am to get the funds I desire. As for leading Bible studies, I was amiss in not gathering the servants for Sabbath worship, but after all, is that a woman's place? We must needs hire a chaplain to conduct them."

" 'Tis plain to see you have neglected your personal devotions, also."

"Aye, to my shame, I have, but I'll wager 'tis easier for you to study in the London townhouse or on shipboard than it is for me on a day when the main chimney is clogged, two servants have the grippe, and Humfrey dumps a dispute between shearers in my lap. You come down here and play the gentleman farmer without ever soiling your hands. Roll up your sleeves and help with the day-to-day labor and see how pious you be! Christ himself took the form of a servant. I think womankind can understand that role far better than menfolk ever will."

Thomas had looked uncomfortable during her tirade, glancing at the door as her voice grew continuously louder. When she paused and began pacing back and forth, he stepped in front of her and put his hand on her shoulders. "Rose, Rose, peace. All these matters that vex you can be amended. 'Tis plain you need more servants.

You mentioned last night that you wished to hire a nurse for Derry. Do so. That should free Sybil for other work. And if you still need more maidservants, then hire them. I'll see that Humfrey troubles you no more about farm matters and supplies all you need from the household accounts."

"If I am mistress of this house, then I wish to control the household accounts," she insisted, brushing away her angry tears. "I learned something of bookkeeping in Joan's mercer shop. I'm not a dunce, you know. If you recall, I helped my brother Robin edit the Protestant pamphlets which we smuggled back into England from Emden."

"Aye, Rose, I recall. You are as intelligent as you are comely," he said soothingly, and she allowed him to wipe her tears with his handkerchief.

"Then why do I feel as if I'm a princess locked in a tower and left alone? Thomas, I want to learn all about your business, and I want to start a venture of my own." She told him about Widow Malorie and her plan to supply needy women with knitting yarn and how she would organize them to sell their goods at markets and fairs.

"A worthy ambition. We just might see about you opening a small shop in London, also."

"Oh, Thomas, could I?" she blurted excitedly. "I wouldn't have to run it myself. I could find a martyr's widow in London. Joan could help—"

"Stay, stay, my whiting," Thomas said with a laugh, "I'll be here with you for the entire month of August. We've plenty of time to make plans. But please, my stomach is crying out. Let's go down to breakfast."

At breakfast, as Thomas discussed the Antwerp Mart with Edmund, he took care to include Rose in the conversation and patiently answered all her questions about the silk trade. Then he drew up documents giving Edmund power as his agent. After signing them, he spilled a bit of melted wax on the foolscap and sealed it with his merchant's ring. "There, done," he said as he handed the documents to Edmund. "Give the one to my agent in London and he'll give you the necessary funds, and present the other letter to the officials at Antwerp." He shook Edmund's hand. "I'm counting on you, my lad. Follow my instructions."

"I shall, sir," assured Edmund. "You may depend on me." He gave a little bow and Rose thought how distasteful was his mock sincerity. She felt uneasy at the thought of his handling Thomas's affairs, and yet she was glad he would be gone.

Edmund took her hand. "My thanks for your hospitality, madam." Rose merely nodded and retrieved her hand as Edmund said to Thomas, "She dined me on King's fare, sir. Oysters in gravy. You must sample the dish, but have a care, lest you burn yourself." With a swirl of his cape, he mounted his horse and putting spurs to him was quickly out of sight.

"Young hotspur," said Thomas affectionately. "Curious in his speech, though. What could he have meant about my getting burned?" Rose gave no answer but began asking Thomas about the wool trade. "You amaze me," he said. "Audrey, from the day we wed, asked not a single question about my business."

"Did she ever travel with you to the Continent?" Rose asked. The image of Thomas traveling with his first wife invoked pangs of jealousy in Rose. *I'm coming to love him more deeply than I realized*, she thought.

"Audrey accompany me? Never. She was content to remain on our manor in Kent, surrounded by her sisters and cousins. I do believe she would not have grieved overmuch if I had never returned."

Rose's jealous feelings vanished like a vapor, and she slipped her hand around Thomas's arm as they went inside.

That afternoon, Rose, Thomas and Derry rode to Widow Malorie's cottage. The widow was overjoyed that they wished to hire Anne as Derry's nurse. Thomas viewed samples of the widow's knitted garments and offered suggestions as to how Rose could best market them. "This cap." He held up a knitted baby cap with an unusual pattern of twists and knots that gave the texture of a garland of flowers about the crown. "If this were made with the finest yarn and subtle shades, it would appeal to some wealthy London matron. Let her display her babe in it at his christening and scores of her peers would seek to buy similar caps. Any cottager can knit a crude garment that will keep a babe warm," he said. "You must concentrate on the unusual and the delicate."

"I have some other patterns that were handed down from my

grandmother," said Widow Malorie, "but I've never had the yarns nor the time to try them."

"Would you share them with other widows?" Rose asked.

"Of course, if it will help," the widow replied.

"Well, you ladies work out the production side of this endeavor," said Thomas. "For my part, when I next return to London, I'll choose a site for the shop and make sure you are not infringing on any guild's territory. The London guilds jealously guard their rights."

Anne had but one gown and a pitiful little kerchief of belongings to bring with her to Grendal Hall. She viewed the hall with round-eyed awe, but was most delighted that she would have her own small featherbed next to Derry's in the nursery. Derry immediately began a game of "ring-of-roses" with her and then grabbed her hand and took her out to see the horses.

As Rose followed them downstairs, she paused by Sybil who was polishing the bannister.

"I—I have engaged a girl, Anne Malorie, to be Derry's nurse," she told her. "—good news for you in that it will give you more time to—uh—"

"Clean the dovecote?" Sybil muttered, and kept polishing.

"Nay, I meant, well—we are going to hire more servants, and you will supervise their work."

Sybil looked up with a self-satisfied smile. Rose bit her lip as she hurried down the stairs and out the door. "Why did I curry that woman's favor?" she asked herself. "She is only a maidservant and now I've told her she will be running the house. Poor Mary takes enough of her bossiness and now I'm going to hire others for her to command and all because I fear her sharp and lying tongue. Oh, well, if Thomas and I grow ever closer while he is on the manor, I'll soon be able to risk his hearing her accusations."

The next day, Joan's messenger arrived with another letter.

A fine thing,—you stuck in the wilderness while your dear husband gads about. Last week I caught a glimpse of him near St. Paul's. He was with that handsome devil, Edmund Laxton, and the men seemed to be enjoying the company of Elinore and Mary Townsley, the twin daughters of Elias Townsley the jewel merchant.

Mark my word, either you must tie your man down or travel

with him. I could always be persuaded to mind Derry here while you traveled.

Speaking of St. Paul's, you may not believe it, but I heard a sermon there in the courtyard. I tried to listen carefully but the preacher prattled on and although he was loud, my bunions were crying out to me even more loudly and I cannot tell you what he said, except that he mentioned hell-fire many times.

Rose, if you and Derry come for a visit, I vow I will listen meekly if you wish to expound the Scriptures for me.

Your friend, Joan

You wiley old dear, thought Rose. First you try to bribe me with laces and now you pretend to want religious instruction. And you shamelessly try to make me jealous as a means of bringing Derry to you. She thought for a moment and then replied.

Dear Friend:

Surely you have better things to do than to spy upon my husband. I appreciate your concern, but I'm certain it was Edmund Laxton and not Thomas who cultivated the young women's friendship. You called Edmund a "handsome devil." An apt description. When I see you I have a tale to tell about that man.

I am joyed to hear that you worshiped at St. Paul's. As for my instructing you, how is it that you never cared to hear me read Scriptures before? However, if you truly wish to know God, you don't need to wait for a visit from me. There are many godly preachers in London who will show you the way and help you to know how to study God's Word for yourself. "Seek and ye shall find," says the Lord.

I think you will be pleased to hear that I too am becoming a woman of business. In order to help poor widows of martyrs, I have encouraged a group of them to construct fine knitted garments which I plan to sell at fairs and in a shop of my own in London. I have one woman, Margaret Malorie, whom I hope to place in charge of it. When I do journey to London, will you help me find a suitable place? Mayhap you will also refer your wealthy patrons.

I look forward to seeing you, but for now Thomas is home and we need to be together. Thomas needs to become better acquainted with Derry. He has never been around children and largely ignores—" (She paused and crossed out the last three words. *No need to strengthen Joan's dislike of Thomas*, she thought.)

This bit of paper I've enclosed decorated with the squiggly lines is Derry's own letter to his Aunty Joan.

Love, Rose.

For the next few weeks life on the manor fell into a happy routine. New servants were hired and the household ran smoothly. The two new maidservants were older women of the village and not upset by Sybil's overbearing manner. Rose laughed when she heard one of them refer to Sybil as "Mistress Jabber-jaws."

Thomas spent his days pretending to supervise the wheat harvest, while Humfrey did his best to keep him out of the hayward's way so that the task could be completed. Rose sought out needy women for her business venture and soon had knitters in Bury, Woolpit and Elmsell working with Margaret Malorie's patterns. Rose supplied the yarns and paid them by the piece, so they would have money to live on until the shop was opened in London. After several days of watchfulness, she was assured that Anne took very good care of Derry. She walked into the nursery one evening and overheard Anne telling the story of baby Moses in the bulrushes, and she was even more confident that she had chosen the proper nurse for her son.

One day while she and Thomas were riding in their own pastureland, they came across a curious circle of stones. "A henge of stones," Thomas explained. "People used them long ago as a sort of altar to heathen gods. Humfrey told me there was one on our land."

"But they don't look as if they've been here very long," Rose observed. She could see a scrape in the earth where one of the larger stones had been pushed into alignment. They dismounted and Thomas kicked at one of them. "Mayhap some children of the tenants have been out here telling ghost stories. In any case, I think I'll have them carted back to the hall. Some of them are quite colorful and could border a path in our garden."

Rose shivered. "Do you think that wise? These very stones might have been drenched with the blood of heathen sacrifices."

Thomas laughed. "What an imagination you have! You could be a minstrel," he teased.

"You mock me, but I can just see the wicked heathen worshipers dancing around this circle in the moonlight, chanting to their gods. I've heard tell they even made human sacrifices at the time of the summer solstice."

" 'Tis people's hearts that are wicked, not stones or other objects. 'Tis how a man uses them and what he puts his trust in." He held up his hand and touched his merchant ring on his finger. "If I use this ring to seal my business documents, I do well. If I believed that since it had been my good father's, the ring contained power to help me get wealth, then I am evil, not the ring."

Rose felt a compulsion to tell him about Sybil and the charm, but again she hesitated. He might berate the maidservant and she would fulfill her threats. She would keep silent a little longer, she decided. Their life was so pleasant of late, she wished to do nothing that would spoil it.

One other thing caused her some concern and that was Thomas's relationship to Derry. Thomas was not used to having children about, and he never spoke directly to Derry. This caused Derry to be uneasy around Thomas so that he began hiding behind Anne's skirts whenever Thomas entered the room.

One day at dinner Rose had Derry do his imitation of a rooster for Anne. Standing up on the bench at the table, the child strutted and crowed. Rose and Anne applauded, and Rose saw Derry glance shyly at Thomas for approval. Thomas was buttering a piece of bread and didn't respond.

"Thomas," Rose chided, "you didn't watch Derry's performance."

"What? Oh, forgive me, my dear. I am unused to playacting at the dinner table."

"But you ignore the child," she persisted. "Can't you at least speak to him?"

"Very well." Thomas put his knife down and stared solemnly at the little boy. Derry edged closer to Anne. "Derry," he began. "Oh, why don't you call him by his given name, Derick? I feel as though I'm beginning a nursery rhyme, Derry dilly down, or something."

"Thomas, you're impossible!" exclaimed Rose as she threw down her napkin and scooped Derry up in her arms. Thomas followed her out to the courtyard.

"Give Derick to me," he demanded.

"Derry, his name is Derry. I'll call him Derick when he is older." Derry clung to her neck and began to cry.

"Give me *Derry*, then!" shouted Thomas above Derry's wailing. "I want to get to know the la—to know Derry, but I feel ill at ease with you watching like a mother hen. We'll go riding, *alone*."

"But his nap—"

"Bother his nap. Do you want me to befriend the child or not?"

"Aye, here." She handed over her son and watched as Thomas carried the sniffling child toward the stables.

She paced the parlor for over an hour. When the German clock on the mantle approached the second hour, she ordered her horse saddled and went out to look for the two. She knew Thomas's stallion was ofttimes hard to handle and with a small crying child upon him, she was afraid the horse might have bolted. Derry and Thomas might be lying injured on a deserted path. She asked a mower if he had seen them and he pointed toward a wooded area in the distance. She knew a peaceful hollow lay beyond the woods where the stream which crossed their land expanded into a quiet pond. She galloped off in that direction, then dismounted and walked her horse through the thick woods. As she neared the hollow she could hear Derry's happy chattering and Thomas's gentle voice. She tied her horse to a bush and softly moved forward. She could see them both squatting down at the edge of the pond with their backs to her. Derry's head was turned up, listening intently as Thomas said, "and then the tadpole lost his tail and grew legs." He held out something in his cupped hands to Derry. "Feel how slippery—"

"Nay!" Derry cried out, losing his balance and tumbling down the muddy bank to the water's edge. He wailed loudly and Rose took a step toward him. She restrained herself just in time as Thomas awkwardly picked the boy up and patted his back.

"There, there, my lad." Derry clung to his neck and stopped crying. "A frog will not harm you. I—Father—will let nothing harm you. Father loves you." Just then Rose's horse whinnied. Thomas turned, startled to see her watching.

"Mama, mama," Derry called to her. "See the frogs? Father won't let them harm us." He still clung to Thomas's neck, and as Rose joined them she made no move to take the boy away from him.

She smiled at Thomas and he looked a little embarrassed, but she was very pleased to see his tenderness with Derry. She would have to remind herself to stand back and give Thomas a chance to learn to be a father. She had been too protective of the boy. "Very well,

Derry," she said. "If Father promises to protect us, I would like to see the frogs." She took Thomas's hand as she knelt down with them beside the pond.

When the harvest was completed, Rose and Thomas presided over a huge harvest feast of roast meats, seed cakes, pastries and frumenty, the traditional dish made with new wheat, milk, eggs and sugar. After all the laborers had eaten their fill, Rose gave them small gifts. She was finally beginning to feel at home on the manor and at ease with her position as its lady.

At dawn Thomas and Rose awoke to an urgent knocking on the bedchamber door. "Who is it?" Rose cried out as Thomas stirred from his pillow.

"Someone for Master," Sybil tersely replied.

"Who can it be—middle of the night—" mumbled Thomas as he hurriedly threw on his clothes.

"No doubt Humfrey and his hogs," Rose murmured, pulling the coverlet up under her chin.

"Hogs?"

"Never mind, dear, an old happening."

Rose was still in bed when Thomas returned to their room. His face was red and his hands were clenched. "Where's my traveling chest? I must pack at once. What a fool I've been!"

"What is it? Where must you go?"

"Antwerp." His voice was shaking with rage. "My messenger reports that Edmund seduced a city official's daughter. When the irate father sent the constables after him, the scalawag left town with all my funds. Another Merchant Adventurer discovered that Edmund hadn't paid any duty on my silks, and they are locked up in a warehouse. 'Twill be a miracle if the officials release them, even if I pay double. This matter will need much diplomacy from me personally if I am to save not only the shipment but my reputation in the exchange mart."

"But how long will you be absent?"

"I cannot say, my dear. Even if I finish my business in a short time, which I doubt, there may not be favorable sailing weather. You and Derry could accompany me," he said tentatively.

Rose shook her head. She was a terrible sailor and she knew it would be almost impossible to keep a little boy not quite three years old from getting into danger aboard a sailing vessel. "Nay, we'll remain here."

"Aye, 'tis best. If you'll see to the packing, I'll go downstairs and give you my power of attorney in case my agents in London or Norwich need a signature." He gestured to the money chest on the court cupboard, "All the funds you might need are in there. Hide it in a safe place."

Just then Derry skipped into their chamber, still in his nightshirt, his black curly hair all tousled. "Morning, Mama, Father." Thomas picked him up.

"Father's going on a long journey, Derry, and he's going to miss you and Mama very much."

Chapter Seven

ROSE WALKED through the gateway of the estate and looked down the road toward the village of Goodthorpe. Several farm workers were trudging homeward in the late afternoon sun. She could see smoke rising from distant cottage chimneys as the housewives prepared their simple suppers. The two village women she had hired as maidservants curtsied to her as they passed by her. They were walking fast, for unlike the men, their labor was not yet finished. They had families to cook for and children to put to bed. Rose envied them. Their husbands could be counted upon to sit each night at their tables and lie each night in their beds.

A soft breeze stirred and swept her along as she turned back toward the hall. She could hear Derry's laughter as he played with Anne in the walled garden, and as she approached the courtyard, she could hear the clatter of pans through the open kitchen windeye. She sighed. Having servants to help with the housework was a pleasure. She had never cared for scrubbing and sweeping, but she missed not having her own kitchen. Bess was a good cook, but only tolerated Rose's presence in her domain and sniffed and muttered if Rose suggested using a different herb or adding an extra ingredient to her dishes.

"Thomas has been absent just a week," she told herself, "and you are as melancholy as a lass whose swain has gone to war." It must be the season, she decided. Harvest time over, time to begin gathering in, making things snug for the coming winter months. She paused and looked at Grendal Hall, its red bricks taking on a burnished glow in the afternoon rays. "What is lacking in me," she mused, "that I do not sing with contentment just to live in such a grand dwelling with my dear son?" She stepped inside and came face to face with Humfrey.

"Mistress Stratton." He bowed and stood aside to let her enter.

"What is it, Humfrey?" She didn't want any problems now.

" 'Tis fair time," he began in his slow, deliberate way.

"A fair at Bury?"

"Nay, the big one, Stourbridge, over't Cambridge way."

Stourbridge. She had heard of that huge fair all her life. Every year during the last three weeks in September the fair was set up in a large field near Cambridge. Sellers from all over the country, including foreign merchants, set up their stalls until the place resembled a large city. Humfrey had paused, waiting for her to prompt him again. "And you wish to journey there?" she asked.

"I do." He rubbed his jaw. "Always do. Lay in the year's supplies."

Suddenly Rose felt excited as a child on market day. Here was an opportunity to prove her skill as a business woman. She would go to the fair herself and buy knitting supplies. "Then you shall go and I'll accompany you."

Humfrey looked aghast at the thought. "More 'n forty mile," he cautioned. "The men and I sleep out-of-doors."

" 'Tis closer than London," she replied, "and I'm sure we can find me suitable lodgings. I'll be ready in the morning."

As she packed that evening, the novelty of the idea had dimmed a little and she began to feel guilty for leaving Derry. *He won't understand, the dearling, but I must assure him that I'll be gone for just a short time.* She went into the nursery and discussed her plans with Anne while Derry played on the floor with his ball.

"I'm sure we will manage splendidly, madam," Anne said. "If there is any problem, I can always send for my mother."

"I've spoken to Bess and she will help you, also," said Rose. Just the day before, Sybil had asked and received permission to visit a distant relative near Stanton. Thomas was not there to protest, and she was grateful the maidservant would be out of the way while she was absent from the manor.

Rose knelt down beside Derry. "Now, dearling, Mama's going away early in the morning, but she'll be back soon with some new toys for you."

"A drum?" he asked, not looking up from his ball. "Some soldiers?"

"Aye, love, whatever you wish."

"Bye-bye," he said nonchalantly, waving his hand. He rolled his ball to Anne.

The trip was not as exciting as Rose had imagined it would be. What joy is there in watching jugglers and acrobats and strolling musicians with no one to share the experience? Every time she saw a mother buying her child some gingerbread or a father lifting his son up on his shoulders to give him a better view of the acrobats, she missed Derry mightily. Still, she reminded herself, the journey was much too long for a small child to make and then turn around and make the journey home in just a few days. Nay, she had done right to leave him at home, although he would have loved to see the dancing bear and choose his own new toys from the many stalls that offered them.

Journeying to Stourbridge Fair had been profitable, for aside from selecting household items to add to Humfrey's list of supplies, she discovered ribbons, unusual laces and ornamental buttons for her "widows' guild" to use in their sewing and knitting. She had seen many baby clothes offered for sale at the fair. They confirmed that the items her women were making were of a better quality and could therefore demand higher prices. She also observed some novel ways to display wares which she would adapt to her own proposed shop in London. After two days of buying, she was impatient to return home but pleased she had learned more about merchanting. She would soon make Thomas proud of her business abilities, she vowed.

Several problems greeted her return to the manor. As Anne was helping her unpack, she gave the girl the key to her jewel casket which she kept in the court cupboard and asked her to replace the few simple necklaces she had taken on her journey. A few moments later Anne gave a startled cry. "Oh, madam, behold, the lock has been broken."

Rose carried the casket to the bed and hastily sifted through the broaches and rings and necklaces. "Nothing has been stolen that I—oh, but this is odd. Look here, Anne, my ruby, the one Thomas gave me as a wedding gift. It's been taken from its own compartment under the false bottom and left here among the things of lesser value." She frowned. "Who could have—"

"Not I, madam, I swear," Anne protested.

"Of course not, dear. It never crossed my mind." Rose patted the girl's hand.

"Why would someone break the lock and then not steal anything?" Anne asked.

Rose considered. "Mayhap the thief heard your footsteps and hastily retreated, or—" Sybil's face flashed in her mind, "or mayhap 'twas someone who just wished to taunt me." *And she'll not get a second chance*, Rose decided. Later that day Rose carefully wrapped the ruby in a bit of velvet and placed it in a small wooden box which she privately asked Humfrey to keep hidden for her.

Her other problem was much more distressing to her. Derry had been pulling away from her refusing to return her hugs and kisses. In fact, he ignored her completely for the first few days, pretending he didn't hear her speak to him, averting his eyes when she entered the nursery, and running to Anne with every little problem.

Rose was so upset she consulted Margaret Malorie about the problem. "The lad's just punishing you for leaving him," the widow told her. "The young ones don't have the words to speak their anger or grief, so they act it out. 'Twill pass. My own children did the same when I once went off a few days to nurse my old auntie."

Rose was relieved that Derry did begin responding to her within a week's time, but he still became concerned whenever she was out of his sight. During the first weeks of October, she watched daily for Thomas's return, until a messenger brought her a letter. "Forgive my delay, my dear Rose," wrote Thomas, "but Edmund did more damage than one could imagine possible. He insulted members of the House of Maiolo from Genoa who supply my firm with all its Mediterranean wares, and then he apparently borrowed money under my name from scores of merchants. It will take me a few more weeks to liquidate assets to reimburse all of them. My thoughts are ever with you. Greet Derry with a kiss from his father. Love, Thomas."

But the days passed and November brought cold and rainy weather. "Wake up, my little man. You're three years old today," Rose called gently on the seventh day of November. As Derry stirred in his bed, Rose drew back the blue curtain from the small mullioned window. She was pleased to see the sun filtering through the panes. "Come, my sleepy head," she said and she lifted him into her arms. "Open those big brown eyes so you can see the gifts I have for you."

"Ready," called Rose, and Anne came in bearing wine-colored velvet garments in her arms. "Look, my dearling, breeches and a doublet just like Father's. No more skirts for you." Derry yelped with glee and eagerly struggled out of his nightshirt. "When Anne has helped you dress, come down into the courtyard and see your other gift," Rose said.

Rose pulled her cloak about her as she waited in the courtyard. *Oh, Thomas, I wish you were here to share this day,* she thought. Just then Anne came out with Derry, resplendent in his manly clothes. Rose bit her lip to keep from laughing at the fierce look on his face and the exaggerated walk. She signaled Tad and he brought out Derry's gift from behind a corner of the Hall.

"A pony, a pony!" Derry shouted with glee. He ran up to the coal-black pony and jumped up and down. "A ride, I want to ride."

Rose glanced up. The clouds had returned and it was getting chilly. "Very well," she agreed, "but just for a moment. She lifted him on the pony and tucked his cape around his legs. "Tad, lead him slowly around the courtyard."

Anne had strolled down the driveway and now came running back. "Oh, madam, there's a tinker at the gate with all kinds of wares to sell. Shall I go inspect his wares? Do we not need a new ladle?"

Rose smiled. A peddler would carry many goods besides ladles and other kitchen tools, things a young girl might fancy: ribbons, laces, sachets, haircombs. Rose fetched a few pence from the purse tied to her kirtle. "Here, my dear, you took such fine care of Derry while I was away. Buy yourself a gift, and tonight, after Derry's abed, we shall cut out a new winter gown for you."

Anne fairly skipped down the winding drive. Rose was grateful not only for her care of Derry, but because she was a good companion on the lonely evenings.

That evening as they began cutting from a bolt of russet woolen, there was a knock on the outer door. Sybil ushered in a young man whose cape dripped with rainwater and whose boots were streaked with mud. "Here, you, not one more step on my clean floor," she heard Sybil scold. "I'll fetch the mistress."

The young man bowed when Rose entered the hallway. He was panting heavily. "Evening, madam, is Master Stratton in? I have an urgent message from my mistress." He paused to catch his breath.

"But who—" Rose began. "Is it Joan Denley?"

"Nay, Mistress Basing of Norwich. The sister of Thaddeus Basing, your husband's agent or I should say, former agent. The gentleman passed away early yesterday morning. She sent me in all haste to notify Master Stratton. She said her brother's dying words were that Master Stratton must see to the payments of the clothiers without delay." He leaned against the wall.

"Here, Sybil, take the lad into the kitchen and feed him, then tell Humfrey to stable his horse and find him a warm place to sleep. My thanks to you—"

"George, madam."

"My thanks to you, George. Your swift execution of your duty shall be rewarded."

"What am I do to?" she thought aloud as she returned to the parlor. "If I send a message down to Thomas's agent in London, 'twill take two days and then another three or four before he could reach Norwich. I have Thomas's power of attorney and could transact whatever business is necessary. Surely this Mistress Basing would know the details. Aye, that's it. I'll ride back with the messenger and a few other men for protection on the road, and I'll take you and Derry along with me, Anne."

"Norwich, I've heard tell it is almost as large as London itself," said Anne. "Me, who's never been farther than Bury—oh," the girl's face fell.

"What is it, dear?"

"I didn't tell you what the peddler said as I was buying laces. A terrible fever has taken some of the folk along the coastline. A foreign ship put in at Yarmouth and its seamen carried the disease ashore."

"Not the plague, God shield us?"

"Nay, but some raging fever."

"I cannot expose Derry to any disease," replied Rose. "Besides, in my haste I hadn't considered the foul weather we're having. You and Derry must abide on the estate. I would let the business go undone in Norwich, but Thomas's reputation has suffered enough from Edmund Laxton's treachery. I must uphold his good name. Anne, do you think you can manage again without me?"

The girl nodded, clearly disappointed.

"Very well. You must promise me," she added in a low voice, "that you and you alone will care for Derry. I don't want Sybil to attend him."

"I promise," said Anne. "And, madam, do not fret. If you wish, Derry and I could stay with my mother."

Rose considered. With so many children scampering about, one of them might contract the fever and give it to Derry.

"Nay, dear, 'tis best if Derry sleeps in his own bed. Your mother has enough work on her hands."

Derry nodded solemnly the next morning as Rose explained that she had to go away again for a few days, but as she mounted her horse in the courtyard, he screamed, "I want to go with you!" and struggled within Anne's arms.

Rose hesitated and her hand slackened on the reins. She was torn between her roles as mother and helpmeet, but, she thought, Derry hadn't really suffered from their first separation, and this journey would show Thomas how much she could aid his work and that she was more than just a housewife. "Mama will return soon!" she shouted over his cries.

"Mama! Mama!" he cried plaintively and arched his back and kicked at Anne. Bess took the struggling boy from Anne. "I'll just take him inside, madam," she called. " 'Tis best if you leave speedily."

"Aye, let us be off, madam," agreed the hayward. " 'Tis a good day's journey to the inn at Diss, and the weather will not hold much longer, I fear."

"Good bye, my love!" she shouted to Derry as Bess carried him up the steps to the door. He stopped his struggling for a second and looked toward her, his arms stretched out to her over the cook's shoulder.

I did not pray. That thought struck her as her eyes met those of her son's. *I didn't even ask the Lord's guidance in making this decision.*

"Madam, please," came the insistent voice of the hayward.

Rose's horse pranced sideways and for a moment she seemed suspended in time. Then she took a firm control of the reins and leaned forward. "Farewell," she called over her shoulder, little realizing that might be the last word her child would ever hear his mother speak.

Chapter Eight

ROSE AND HER escorts reached the town of Diss, halfway to Norwich, by nightfall. Just as they entered the crowded inn, it began to rain heavily. The men had to bed down on the floor of the public room, while Rose shared a tiny bedchamber with another female traveler who was already snoring loudly when Rose got into bed. Rose covered her ears and tried to pray, but her petitions seemed to reach no further than the low ceiling of the bedchamber. After tossing and turning for a time, she decided to get up and read her Bible by the light of the dying embers in the hearth. She rummaged through her things in the traveling chest, but couldn't find the book.

I didn't even pack the Bible. For shame, she chided herself. *Thomas was right to upbraid me. How easy it is to neglect my devotions when life runs smoothly*. With a sigh she returned to bed and fell asleep counting the other woman's snores and dreamed of being chased by monsters whose noses were silver trumpets.

The next morning was clear and the old Roman road leading northeast from Diss was easy to travel in spite of the recent rain. The party made good time and arrived at the walled city of Norwich late that afternoon. As they approached the gate, a man wielding a staff barred their way.

"Stand aside, man, my lady has business in your town," ordered the hayward.

The gatekeeper stood his ground. "Be you from London?" he asked.

"Nay, we come from Suffolk near Bury, if it's any of your concern."

" 'Tis. We've heard of a plague a-brewing in London and we will not have travelers bringing it here."

"Sir, we've had no word of a plague in London," said Rose, "although I did hear rumor of a fever in Yarmouth." She dismounted and walked up to the guard. "I'm Mistress Stratton. My husband has business holdings in Norwich. I've come because of the death of my husband's agent, Thaddeus Basing. Perhaps you've heard of him?"

The gatekeeper relaxed and gave Rose a bow. "Your servant, madam. Of a truth I knew Master Basing. My neice, Blanche, is his scullery maid. Pass by then, and welcome."

It was nearing dusk as they rode into Norwich. The graying light cast shadows from the crowded rows of houses across the narrow cobblestone streets. Rose had the odd feeling that she was riding into a prison. She shivered and reached for the silver gilt pomander which hung as a pendant on her girdle, but even the scent of the nutmeg within could not hide the odor of raw sewage. She was tired, she missed Derry, and she wondered for the hundredth time if she had done right to leave him at the manor.

They followed a street which wound around a meadow, rimming a large mound. On the mound sat a huge fortress. "A castle?" she asked George, the messenger who was guiding them.

"Mayhap in olden days, but in my remembrance it has always been a prison."

Rose shuddered. She well knew what the prisoners inside were suffering. The smells that assaulted her in the streets were nothing compared to a dank and crowded cell. She uttered a silent prayer for all the captives inside and made a mental note to send bread to the prisoners.

On Elm Hill, an elderly porter opened the gate to the small courtyard of the house where Basing lived. The house was L-shaped, the main portion lying parallel to the street and the side wing running toward the street. Rose was greeted at the door by Mistress Basing, a delicate wisp of a woman who looked about sixty.

"I sorrow with you at the loss of your brother," Rose said as the older woman showed her into the parlor.

Mistress Basing's fragile hands fluttered in her lap like fallen leaves stirred by the wind. "He was a dear man," she said, "and he conducted your husband's business affairs as carefully as if they were his own. He could not rest until I assured him that I would send for your husband at once. 'Rest, dear,' I told him. 'Close your eyes and rest,' and I kissed him on his forehead, and he was gone." She was silent for a moment and then looked up with alarm, "But your husband, has he not accompanied you? He must come, the clothiers—" Rose explained Thomas's absence and was taken to the counting house where Mistress Basing showed her the books her brother kept.

"I'm afraid my brother had his own method of keeping books." She opened one and Rose saw columns written in a spidery hand, full of strange abbreviations. "I told him to hire an apprentice to teach, but he didn't want to squander your husband's money. Three clothiers who sell worsted cloth to the firm came the next morning after my brother passed away and demanded their money." She handed Rose a sheaf of paper. "I had them put it in writing, although I cannot read."

Rose spent hours poring over the books that night, trying to decipher Basing's entries. She finally gave up and decided just to trust the men's account of what was owed them. Adding the three amounts up, however, she found she was short twenty-three pounds of having enough to pay them all.

When she told Mistress Basing, the lady showed Rose a chest which contained various silver gilt items. "My brother kept these to sell when ready cash was needed. Those clothiers like to be paid on the nail, he would say."

"Oh, but I couldn't take the plate that is rightfully yours," said Rose.

"Nay, dear, the house and its furnishings all belong to Master Stratton. These are yours to do with as you wish. I'll be finding a place to stay on the morrow."

"Please abide here," Rose stated, "and care for the dwelling until my husband returns from abroad and secures another agent."

"You are most kind, madam."

Rose tossed fitfully on her bed that night. Surely she could sell the plate and pay off the clothiers tomorrow and then set off for the manor the next day. *I shall not leave Derry again*, she promised herself.

Two of the clothiers showed up on her doorstep the next morning and she quickly paid them and sent the hayward out with George to offer a silver salt cellar, a nest of gilt bowls and twelve silver spoons to a Norwich merchant. The other clothiers told her that the third had journeyed to his estate and would return for his payment the next day.

Another day before I can leave for home, she fumed. But it was a beautiful day and she decided to spend the afternoon exploring the city and shopping for gifts for Derry and Thomas. It was market day in Norwich and the hours passed quickly as Rose browsed in shops, walked beside the River Wensum and inspected the beautiful Cathedral. She purchased a riding whip for Thomas and a jack-in-the-box and book of ABC's for Derry. "He is so intelligent for his age," she mused. "I can soon begin teaching him to read and write."

Rose was happily carrying her purchases down a narrow lane when she realized she had lost her way. She could see the spire of the Cathedral to her right, but as she turned around to look for another landmark, she stumbled and broke the heel of her left shoe. A woman tapped her on the shoulder and pointed down the lane to a sign with the picture of a boot and "T. Wooten, Cobbler."

As she entered the cobbler's shop, she observed how different it was from her friend Barnabe's in Boxton. His shop had been neat and tidy; here everything was lying about—tools, shoes to be mended, scraps of leather. The cobbler looked up from his bench and approached her. He was as unkempt as his shop. His salt and pepper beard was untrimmed and a blob of dried egg yolk nested in it. "Good day, madam, and how may I serve you?" he asked, scrutinizing her head to toe as if assessing to the pence how much he would charge her.

She disliked him immediately and if she had known the whereabouts of another cobbler would have turned around and exited. She held up the heel that had broken off.

"Sit here, my lady," he beckoned, sweeping a pile of leather scraps off a bench. "I shall repair your shoe with all speed. Colin," he bellowed, "some ale! May I offer you refreshment?" his voice changed to sickly sweet tone. Rose shook her head.

A pale, thin boy about twelve years old brought the cobbler a mug of ale. Although it was cold in the shop there were beads of perspiration on the boy's forehead and above his upper lip.

"Are you ill, lad?" Rose asked gently. He stared at her and Rose wondered if that was the first gentle speech he had heard. He shook his head and his chin quivered as if he were about to cry.

"Boy," growled the cobbler, "bring me the ale and get back to your work."

"But can you not see the lad's ill?" asked Rose.

"Ill? Bah, he's a lazy, half-witted nurse child that the parish pays me to keep," replied the cobbler. "But 'tis little pay for all he eats. Here's your shoe, madam. That will be three pence."

After she paid him Rose held out another coin and said, "I fear I have lost my way. May I pay your appren—" the cobbler's scowl made her amend her offer. "May I pay you to allow your apprentice to escort me to Elm Hill?"

The cobbler snatched the coin and nodded. "See you return straightway," he told the boy and turned away.

Colin gave Rose a fleeting smile and hurried outside. The afternoon sun was mild and yet he shielded his eyes against the light. "Come, madam," he said in a weak voice; he began to walk quickly as if eager to get away from his master's sight, but when he rounded a corner, he paused long enough to catch his breath and steady himself on the wall of the shop and then he walked slowly on.

"So you are a nurse child, Colin?" Rose asked. "How long ago did your parents die?"

He shrugged and walked on.

"I, too, was orphaned," she told him, and he looked up at her in disbelief. Now she realized why this boy had so touched her heart. He was about the age her brother Robin had been when the two of them were orphaned in London. That was when her aunt came to take her to her farm near Boxton and left Robin apprenticed to a cruel printer.

They soon reached Elm Hill and she found her house. "Oh, madam, do you own this fine place?" Colin asked as he looked up at the carved door and the three stories. "Aye, lad," she replied.

"My husband and I do. Come inside and I'll have the cook give you a good meal before you leave."

"But my master—"

"I'll give you another coin to pay your master for your delay. Now tell me, what is the lane where your master works?"

Tomorrow, before she left, she would see about persuading the parish officials to let her take Colin in her care. She would do it for Robin's sake.

The boy was fed and scurried off. The hayward and the messenger returned with the money from the sale of the plate and Rose spent the evening trying to decipher Basing's books again to see if there was any other pressing business. She could find nothing. She had enough money left over to leave with Mistress Basing for her and the servants' provisions until Thomas hired an agent. Then she retired, happily looking forward to her trip home.

"Get out, get out, I say!" Rose was awakened by the strident shouts of the old porter. She threw a shawl over her nightgown and went into the gallery. "What is it?" she called down to a maidservant who was standing by the open door.

"Oh, madam, 'tis the young boy you fed last night. He's lying in the courtyard and there's bloody foam coming out of his mouth. The porter's trying to drive him away, but he dare not touch him. He might have the mad dog disease."

"Tell the porter to leave him alone. I'm coming down." Rose hurriedly dressed and by the time she reached the courtyard the entire household was gathered around the boy. "Away, away," she ordered and knelt down by Colin. There were just flecks of blood on his face and shirt and he was holding his sides as he coughed. He looked up at her with glazed eyes as she felt his forehead. His skin was burning to her touch.

"He has no mad dog disease," she said. "Mayhap he's taken some sort of lung fever. Send for a physician," she ordered the porter. "And you," she said to the cook, "help me get him inside."

"Not I, Madam," said the cook. "He might have the plague. You'd best have him carted to the pest house outside the gates of the city." She wiped her hands with her apron. "And to think he sat at my kitchen table and drank out of our cup."

"Stand aside, then," Rose ordered impatiently, "and I'll carry him." But the hayward came up and lifted the boy in his arms. "Where to, Mistress Stratton?" he asked.

"We'll put him in the undercroft." She looked at the other servants. "That should be far enough away from yourselves. At least, can one of you make haste to fix a pallet for him there?" Grudgingly the scullery maid preceded them and made a bed of old blankets in the stone cellar.

Mistress Basing came down the stairs with some candles. "They said—oh, poor child," she murmured. "He must have crept into the courtyard and hidden in the shadows until the porter closed the gate last night. I'll wager his master threw him out when he realized how sick he was—to avoid the burial fee, you know."

"Please, he'll hear you," Rose whispered as she pulled a coverlet over him.

"My pardon," said the older woman, "but I fear the lad is past all hearing." She placed a candle on the storage chest beside the pallet and retreated. As Rose wiped Colin's face with her handkerchief, the elongated shadows made by the candlelight hovered on the walls and vaulted ceiling of the undercroft like eery mourners.

The boy began tossing feverishly. Rose laid her hand on his shoulder. "Lie still, my lad, the physician is on his way."

He jerked his head, "M—don't hit—" He held his hands up and then opened his eyes, "Oh, madam, 'tis you." He made an effort to sit up, but he began coughing, and fresh flecks of blood spattered Rose's hand and her lace handkerchief as she put his head in her lap. *He is dying*, she realized. She stroked his head and when the coughing subsided, asked softly, "Colin, do you know the Lord Jesus Christ? Are you trusting in the Son of God?"

"I'm no man's son," he gasped. " 'Born in an alley—bastard child,' master says,—'child of a whore—no good.' "

"Oh, my dear, sweet child, none of us is good. The Scriptures say, 'There is none righteous, no not one.' That is why our heavenly Father sent His only Son to die for our sins. Colin, you can have that life forever with Jesus if you confess that you are a sinner and accept Christ as your Savior."

"Mistress," called the cook from the stairway, "the physician is attending the Lord. May—'' She was stopped by Rose's uplifted hand and retreated upstairs.

"Colin," Rose continued, "do you confess that you're a sinner?"

He nodded and clutched her hand tightly as a spasm of coughing gripped him, and then he asked in a whisper, "Will He save me?"

"Oh, most gladly. He loves you so much, dear Colin. Now you follow my prayer." He coughed and she said, "You needn't struggle to repeat the words aloud; just think them in your heart. God will hear you. "Dear Lord," she began, "I know I'm a sinner and that you died to redeem me. I repent of my sin and ask you to forgive me and come into my heart and save me. In Jesus' name, amen."

"Amen," whispered Colin. She patted his head as he struggled for breath.

"Don't fear, my lad, don't fear," she whispered soothingly.

"—not afraid," he gasped, "not now—He's here," he said, and with a look of joyous surprise, lifted himself up on his elbows, "He's—" he sighed a long breath and lay back on her lap and was still.

With a sob Rose lay his head gently down on the pallet and closed his eyes. Her tears fell on his emaciated form as she folded his hands across his chest and then covered his face.

"He's dead?" called the cook loudly from the stairs.

Rose merely nodded and the servant scurried up the stairs. Blinded by tears, Rose felt her way up the stairs and then wiped her eyes and went up to her bedchamber and knelt down by the bed. "Oh, Father, oh, Father, the sorrows in this wicked world," she prayed. "The children with no love nor care, the prisoners with no hope. Oh, forgive me, Lord. I have not shared your light as I should. I've been so selfish of late, so occupied with my own welfare." She looked down at the lace handkerchief spotted with Colin's blood which she still clutched in her hand. "You spared my life for a purpose and I haven't sought to know that purpose and do it. Teach me, Lord, teach me."

It was as if a floodgate were opened in her heart and she poured out prayer to the Father, not just for herself or Derry and Thomas but for Joan and Widow Malorie and countless others. She felt a precious closeness to God that she hadn't felt since she had been confined in prison. Time stood still as she prayed until a knock on the bedchamber door intruded upon her worship. Mistress Basing was calling, "Madam, come quickly!"

Chapter Nine

MISTRESS BASING was outside her chamber and whispered when she opened the door. " 'Tis the searchers, madam, the old women that the parish officials hire to search among the sick for signs of plague. I suspect the cook sent for them. She's so fearful that the lad had a deadly disease. These two crones are so sotted with drink, they could hardly stagger up the front steps. I've told them the lad is dead but they still insist on viewing the body."

Rose went down into the parlor where the two searchers waited. Both were dressed in garments so filthy that it was impossible for Rose to guess their original hues. One was thin and humpbacked with yellowed skin. She looked as if she were ready for the grave herself. The other was round and florid, her body swollen with unhealthy looking fat.

"Good day, madam," said the thin one. "We've come to view the dead 'un." She looked around with rheumy eyes. "My, what a wondrous fair house."

"Indeed," chimed the other in a raspy voice. "A pity we were not allowed in when Basing died. A high and mighty physician ruled on the cause of his death." She looked around slowly as if taking inventory. Her glance finally rested on the two silver gilt mugs which sat on the mantle piece. The other peered closely at a painted wall hanging.

"Blanche," Rose called to the scullery maid, "escort the searchers down to view the lad." She felt it was her duty to accompany the women, but she couldn't bear the sight of Colin's thin, pale form again. Rose sat in the parlor for quite a while until the searchers and the maid returned. Blanche was red-faced and looked to Rose as if she might explode with anger.

"A pitiful sight," said the fat searcher, huffing from climbing the stairs.

"Woeful, indeed," chimed the other. She squinted in Rose's direction. "Dirty work, it is, to see such sad sights. Fair tears at the heart. We could do with a spot of ale to cheer us up."

"Tell me, what caused the lad's death?" Rose demanded.

"After we've had our ale, dearie," replied the fat one, lowering her head in a stubborn expression which increased the number of her chins.

"Very well. Blanche, fetch them some ale."

Blanche gave Rose a tight-lipped look and flounced into the kitchen. Curious, Rose followed her. "What has angered you?" she asked the servant as she poured the ale.

"Oh, madam, 'twas shameful how they handled the poor lad's body, poking at it and giggling. Lewd women they are. The things they said. Oh, but you'd best not leave them alone in the parlor." Rose hurried in just as the thin one was slipping one of the gilt mugs under her shawl.

"Put that back!" Rose ordered. Blanche came in with the ale. "Forget those," she told Blanche as the women reached for their drinks. Blanche pivoted toward the kitchen, and Rose again addressed the searchers, "Now tell me the cause of death before I send for the constable."

"Oh, 'tis not you who will send for the constable," rasped the fat searcher. "We could have made a favorable report but now—"

"But now, you'll wish you had given us both silver mugs," hissed the thin one as they made for the door.

Idle threats, thought Rose as she watched the two women leave. She sent for the porter and asked him to make arrangements for the boy's funeral and burial. Then with a sigh she went back down to the undercroft to view Colin again. His arms were askew and his shirt pulled up over his head. As she bent to straighten his clothing she noticed the many bruises on his chest. His ribs stood out and several of them appeared broken. "Oh, my dear child!" she exclaimed, "You didn't die of disease; you were beaten to death!" She thought of Wooten the cobbler and wondered how long he had abused the boy. The coroner must be informed. She would tell the porter to fetch him when he returned.

As she went upstairs, the last clothier arrived for his payment. Rose took him to the counting room and paid him in full. He was a talkative man and eager to help her decipher Basing's account books. *Probably curious about Thomas's dealings with other merchants*, Rose thought, but she could not be discourteous to him and so an hour passed before she was rid of him. When she had showed him to the door, the porter was coming up the steps.

"Good, you're back," she told him. "Now you can send for the constable to report—"

"Madam," he broke in, "there's no need to send for him. He is outside the gate with one of his men demanding to see you."

Perhaps the searchers told him of Colin's abused body, she thought. "Then bid them enter," Rose told him.

"I'm glad you've come," she told the constable, noticing a hammer which the other man carried and idly wondered if they planned to build a coffin on the spot to convey the lad's body.

"Are you, indeed? Now there's a strange thing," replied the constable as he gave his assistant a knowing look.

"I'll show you the poor child. Follow me," said Rose as she turned to enter the house.

"Stay, madam. We cannot enter. Have your servants bring out the body in a sheet and lift it into the coffin in our cart outside. We'll take it to be burned."

"Burned! But I am willing to pay for a decent burial."

"There's no burial for a body full of plague."

"Plague? He didn't die of plague. You've just to look at the bruises on his body. He died from ill treatment by his master. All you must do is look at him."

The constable stood his ground. "All I know is what the parish clerk told me. The searchers said they saw signs of plague and we will take no chances. Now send out the body."

Those wicked women, she thought. *Bribery was their game and I didn't play.* "George, Tom, do as he says."

George and the hayward brought out the lifeless form and holding the ends of the sheet tossed it into the cart.

"Constable, please take just one glance at the lad's bruised body. I'm sure—"

"Now do you have bread enough for two weeks to sustain you during the quarantine?" the constable asked, ignoring her request.

"This is most unjust—I know not—"

"Yes, we do," answered Mistress Basing, who had been standing behind Rose. "Surely you will allow us to use our own well in the garden?"

"Aye. But, Ned," he told his helper, "see that the garden gate is boarded up." The man nodded and began hammering the wooden cross on the door on which were painted the words, "Lord have mercy upon us."

"Now all of you, get inside and I warn you I am posting a guard outside your property. There are stiff penalties for anyone breaking quarantine. Is all your household present?" he asked Rose. She looked around.

"Aye, all are here," said Mistress Basing before Rose could speak.

"Very well. Inside with you. And then, Ned, close them in."

They all went inside and listened as Ned nailed boards across the doorway.

The cook was hysterical; Mistress Basing shoved her into the kitchen and sent the hayward and George to count the supplies. "Oh, what am I going to do? I cannot stay here another two weeks," Rose told Mistress Basing. "My son will think I am never coming back. That boy was not ill; he was injured. If only someone on the outside could help us prove it—"

"Shh, come away from the door, madam. There is someone— Blanche, the scullery maid. I had just sent her out to market before the Constable came. My bedchamber windeye looks out upon the street. Hasten, we must watch out it and signal Blanche before the guard sees her or she attempts to enter the courtyard."

Rose followed the older woman upstairs and together they watched the street below for about half an hour until they saw Blanche approach, carrying a basket of bread. She paused as she saw the guard at the courtyard gate, but he gave her no notice. Mistress Basing softly opened the windeye and whistled, giving a credible imitation of a dove. The girl glanced up. Mistress Basing waved and put her hand to her lips. Then she gestured for the servant to go round to the lane outside the garden wall.

When Rose and Mistress Basing reached the garden, the older woman called out softly, "Blanche, are you there?"

"Yea, madam," said the servant. "But why is a guard at our gate?"

Mistress Basing explained briefly and then said, "Listen carefully. Go to your uncle, the gatekeeper, and tell him the searchers came and gave false testimony. Tell him the boy was apprenticed to Wooten, the cobbler on Pottergate street. Tell him that if he can get evidence that the boy died from abuse, not illness, and prove it to the coroner, he shall be paid handsomely. Can you remember all that, girl?"

"Aye, madam, I'll remember."

"Then be gone before the guard—"

"Here, what are you doing, girl?" a man's gruff voice asked. "Do you not know this house is quarantined?"

"Aye, I heard, sir. That is why my mother sent me with some bread for the poor souls."

"Well, then toss that loaf over the wall and be on your way!"

All evening, Rose paced up and down the bedchamber. *How foolish of me to play the business woman, rushing off and leaving my son. Now I am a prisoner in my own lodging.* She slept fitfully and in the morning went downstairs to a commotion in the kitchen.

"Look there and there, these spots on my arm—*plague*. I'm going to die, I know it!" whined the cook.

"Nonsense, you ninny," replied Mistress Basing. "Those marks on your arm are not signs of plague; they're flea bites. You'd be wiser to spend your time turning out your bed and laying it over with wormwood than looking for signs of illness."

"Why is Blanche free to walk about and not us?" asked the porter.

"Be grateful she is outside and can help to lift the quarantine," replied the hayward.

Although the day was gray and cold, Rose spent most of it in the garden, hoping for a word from Blanche. *It would be a lovely garden in the springtime*, she thought, with the trees turning green and flowers blooming in the now barren beds. She thought of the two years of her imprisonment.

After Derry had been born and spirited away by Joan, the endless days had been infinitely more colorless and drab than this garden. How she had awaited messages then. Just a single sentence from Joan smuggled in a loaf of bread or in the wrapping of a square of dried beef would bring her such joy. The first such message she received several months after Derry's birth. "He laughed today," was all it said, and yet it said so much more. Her child was alive; he was safe and healthy and growing. She looked up at the cloudy sky and recalled the first time she had been allowed to exercise in a small prison courtyard. How beautiful the sky had looked to her. *Do things have to be taken away for a while before they can be appreciated?* she wondered.

There was no word that day and it wasn't until two more days when she was about to give up that she heard a clink by the far wall in the garden. She found a rock with a bit of paper tied to it. "Evidence found," it read.

The next afternoon the constable came and removed the sign and boards from the door. "The quarantine has been removed by order of the coroner," he said. The gatekeeper had accompanied him and waited until the constable was gone before he told Rose, "I had to spend two evenings at an alehouse on Pottergate Street until I got the information. Finally, after a few mugs with the shopkeeper next door to Wooten, I learned that he and two others had observed Wooten beating the boy the evening before he died. One had seen Wooten kick the lad in the ribs and threatened to call the constable then. When he had asked where the boy was the next day, Wooten told him he had sent him off to another cobbler, and the shopkeeper thought no more about it. Treats his own apprentice not much better, I ween. Anyway, with a little promise of silver the shopkeeper supplied me with the names of the other two witnesses. The coroner interviewed all three of them. Their testimony along with the fact that there have been no other cases of plague in Norwich for many months caused them to lift the quarantine."

Rose gratefully gave a worthy reward to the gatekeeper and began preparations to return home.

Chapter Ten

THERE WAS NO ONE to greet Rose as she rode alone into the courtyard of Grendal Hall. Sybil, who was laying a fire in the parlor, looked up at her blankly as she entered and then went back to her work, but Bess came out, drying her hands on her apron, "Oh, Mistress, I'm so glad you're back. Little Derry has taken a fever. Some childhood disease, I'm certain, but he has been calling for you. We had planned to send for a—"

Rose bounded up the stairs to the nursery. The curtains were drawn and there was just a little light from a stub of a candle flickering in a pool of melted wax on the clothes chest. Both Anne and Derry were asleep, Derry in his bed and Anne slumped beside it, her hand on Derry's.

"Anne, Anne," Rose whispered, gently shaking the girl's shoulder.

Anne awoke and stood up weakly. "Oh, madam, I didn't hear you come in." She rubbed her eyes. "I was up with Derry all night."

"But what is it? What ails my son?"

"A fever of some sort. It took him of a sudden two nights ago. He tosses and turns, and ofttimes holds his head in pain. He cried so after you left for Norwich. At first I thought it was just inward grief and would pass. Bess said it might be the beginning of chin cough or the scarlet skin that afflicts the young, but he's had no such signs." The young girl swayed on her feet.

"I hope that woman from London didn't infect Master Derry with some dreadful disease."

"Woman from London? Was it Joan Denly?"

"That might have been her name, madam. Tall, she was, and very demanding, but Sybil didn't let her near the child."

Joan—if only she were here now, thought Rose.

"She left a letter. I placed it in your bedchamber."

"I can't bother with it now." Rose gently touched the young girl's hand.

"Go downstairs and refresh yourself," Rose told her. "I'll tend to my son." She knelt by his bed and touched his head. "Derry, Derry, lad," she called softly. " 'Tis Mama, Mama's home." He stirred, but when he barely opened his eyes they were glazed and unseeing. She held her face close to his. "Wake up, sleepy head." He tried to speak but his lips were cracked and bleeding. He lifted his arms weakly up to her. She scooped him up and felt his body burning through the heavy nightshirt he wore. He was limp as a newborn as she sat him in her lap on the bed. She held him tightly and with one hand moistened her handkerchief in the water jug on the bedstand. She dabbed his lips. " 'Tis all right now. You'll be all right," she said soothingly. "Mama will care for you."

But inwardly she was fighting panic. What should she do for him? She had never nursed him through an illness. In the months since she was released from prison and reunited with her son, he hadn't been ill, just an occasional bout of catarrh. She looked at his cracked lips. His breath was hot and smelled of metal. *Liquid, he must have liquids.* She carried him to the doorway. "Anne, Bess, someone fetch me a mug of warm cider and a spoon for Derry."

"You should starve a fever, madam," the cook called up.

"Cider, and quickly!" she ordered. Her common sense told Rose the child needed liquids. It also told her that Derry was far more sick than the servants realized. *If I had been here, instead of playing at merchanting, I would not have allowed this illness to take such a hold on him*, she thought. What did the servants know? She was his mother and she would heal him. *Nay, forgive me, Lord. Only you can heal, but oh, Father, I beg of you, spare Derry's life. Show me what to do.*

The cider was brought. "Here, love," she coaxed, "your favorite drink." She brought the spoon to his lips which were slightly parted.

He took fast shallow breaths. She let one drop of cider spill into his mouth. He didn't respond. "Oh, please, please drink." She let another drop into his mouth and this time he opened his eyes and moved his mouth. Again she tried and he actually swallowed but his tongue and mouth were so dried out that the action caused him pain. He whined pitifully and turned his head away from the spoon. "Good lad, now rest for a moment." *Moisture, he must have more moisture.*

Suddenly she thought of the little hollow and the stream where Thomas had shown Derry the frogs that happy day in August. She felt an urge to take him to that spot. Mayhap the moist air by the stream would soothe him. She knew that if he remained there in the nursery, he would surely die.

Anne came back upstairs. "I'm sorry he took fever, madam," she said, with tears in her eyes. "I tried to care for him properly, but he missed you so and he wouldn't eat—"

Rose noticed the deep circles under the girl's eyes. Her pale skin seemed almost transparent. "You did the best you could, dear," Rose comforted her. "Now help me a bit longer and then you can lie down and rest. Fetch a carrying costrel and pour some of this cider into it." Anne brought her the little stone container and carefully filled it with cider and corked it. Rose took it from her and slung its leather strap over her shoulder. "Now help me wrap Derry in this comforter."

"Are you carrying him into Bury for a physician?"

"Nay," Rose replied. "There's not time for that. Have Tad saddle my horse quickly."

She rode as fast as she could into the wooded area, now a dreary place with most of the trees barren of leaves, except for an occasional bit of green holly. She slipped off her mount with Derry in her arms and almost lost her balance. As she carried him to the hollow, her feet swished through the layers of dead leaves as if they were snow. Thick thorn bushes edged the bank. As she made ready to lay him down at the waterside, her gown caught on a thorn and she stumbled and dropped the child. "Oh, Derry, have I hurt you?" she cried.

He sat up and began moaning. She turned to free her skirt from the bush. "Mama's so sorry. Here let me—" She turned back to Derry, but he had stood up and was walking in a daze toward the water. "Stop! You'll fall—" She yanked at her skirt again and it tore free. "I'll—" She looked toward the water and screamed. Derry was floating facedown in the stream!

She lunged down the bank and into the stream and picked him up. He began choking and sputtering. She turned him over and he was able to take a breath, but he threw his arms about her neck and clung to her so fiercely that her trembling legs gave way and she sat down in the cold stream. He screamed and tried to climb out of the water. "I've got you, I won't let you fall," she soothed and tried to calm herself down. As she patted his back she noticed how much cooler his skin felt. She splashed water on her own face and then, despite his protests, bathed his face and sprinkled water on his head.

At last she felt calm enough to stand up. The weight of her wet gown pulled as she got to her feet and dragged herself up to the grassy verge. Fortunately the comforter had fallen off when she dropped Derry and so she stripped him and wrapped him in its warmth. Holding him and crooning to him, she was overjoyed to see him much more alert and eager to drink the cider. "You're going to be fine," she told him, "just fine. Now we'll go home." She didn't have the strength to mount again, so she began walking toward the manor house. A farm worker spotted her as she came out of the woods and carried the child into the house. Anne held Derry on her lap by the fire in the parlor while Rose changed.

"He feels so much cooler," Anne said when she returned. "Aye, I believe God is healing him," replied Rose. "It was no whim of chance that made me think of taking him to the stream. Whether the shock of the icy water revived him or just cooled his burning skin, it was the turning point."

With much coaxing she was able to feed Derry a little chicken broth that evening, and she watched over him carefully as he slept beside her in the great bedchamber. Although she felt his head often, the fever did not rise again. Every time he stirred she gave him some liquid, either broth or cider. Early in the morning, she thought she felt the fever rise a little, so she bathed him in warm water and he was well enough to fight her all the way. Both of them fell asleep after that ordeal. When she awoke and pulled back the curtain, she judged it must be midmorning. She glanced over at Derry and was startled by the stillness of his little form. She ran to his side and put her ear to his lips, but he was breathing, slowly and regularly. *Praise God*, she thought. *He passed the crisis. He will live.* It was all she could do to keep from waking him and hugging him, but she knew sleep would be his best medicine now. She even felt confident enough to leave him for a moment and go downstairs.

"Is he—?" asked Anne.

"He's fine, just fine," Rose replied. "No fever and he is sleeping soundly. Have Sybil remove all the linen from his sickbed and burn it. Whatever afflicted him must not have a chance to reinfect his body." Rose instructed the cook to make some beef broth and took some bread and cheese for herself back up to the chamber. She noticed the letter from Joan that had been lying on top of the clothes chest all this time, but with a sigh of exhaustion she shoved it into her portable writing desk. *I'll read it and send her a message when Derry has fully recovered*, she thought.

For the next few days she stayed by his side. He would sleep for hours and then wake up for a while. She gradually added bits of bread to his broth, and though he soon ate eagerly, he was still not himself. "It troubles me," she told Anne, "how he will begin to speak and then stop and look puzzled."

"Mayhap his throat is still tender."

"Aye, that must be it." Rose began anticipating his every need to spare him using his voice. Still another worry nagged at her. She would often enter the room and call to him, but he would ignore her completely. At other times he would hug her affectionately. *He's punishing me, just as he did the time I returned from Stourbridge Fair, that's all,* she mused.

But as the days passed and Anne helped more with his care, she too noticed a change in Derry. When she voiced her concern, Rose refused to talk about it. "He is punishing you also," she told Anne. But her secret fear was that his brain had been damaged in some way by the fever. One sunny day she carried him out to the garden and he squealed when he saw a meadow mouse and made some unintelligible sounds as he chased it across the garden. *Mayhap he's forgotten how to speak*, she thought. When he ran up to her and pointed to where the mouse had escaped through a chink in a brick, she grabbed both his hands and said clearly, "The mouse. The mouse has crawled through the wall. Can you say mouse?'' He looked at her and then pulled his hands from her grip and began pounding her legs with his fists.

"Here, you rapscallion," said Anne as she picked him up. "Is that any way to treat your mother who has spent these weeks caring for you?" He struggled to get out of her grasp. "Nay, my lad, you're going for a nap." Rose watched the two leave the garden with a sinking feeling in her stomach. Something was very wrong. If only Thomas were here. Sometimes his calm manner infuriated her, but she wished he were here now to assure her. She had received no message from him since her return from Norwich.

That afternoon Humfrey brought her a fluffy white kitten. "For Master Derry," he said. "I hope the lad is fully recovered from his illness."

"Fully, and thank you," she replied. For once she was more taciturn than he. She didn't wish to speak of Derry's illness anymore. *God has healed him, hasn't He? And doesn't the Lord complete His every work?* she reasoned. *He is fully recovered then.*

She carried the kitten up to the nursery. Through the open door she saw Derry sitting on the floor with his back to her, rolling a ball to Anne.

"Derry, Derry, look what I have," Rose said softly.

He didn't turn around. Anne started to point toward her, but Rose motioned her to stop. "See the pretty kitty?" she said more loudly. Still no response from Derry as he twirled the yellow wooden ball around. With her heart racing she set the kitten on the floor and it began mewing and scampered toward Derry. It ran up and pounced on the twirling ball. Derry made a grab for the little kitten and then stood up and chased it toward Rose. "Kiddah, kiddah," he called in a monotone.

Rose reached down and picked up the kitten. Kneeling in front of her son, she stroked the kitten as she asked, "What shall we name kitty?" Again there was no response. He gently patted the kitten's back with his chubby little hand, and she let him hold it. Rose's heart was pounding now as she cupped her hand under Derry's chin and forced him to look at her as she shouted, "The name, tell me its name or I shall spank you!"

Derry pulled away in fright and began to cry. Rose stood up. "Very well, I shall take the kitten away until you obey." As she grabbed the kitten too tightly around its middle, it dug its claws into Derry causing him to scream with pain. Anne came toward them, "Mistress, please—"

But Rose yanked the kitten from Derry and ran to her bedchamber. She set the kitten down and leaned against the closed door, trembling with emotion. *He's not deaf—he cannot be deaf*—she shook her head. *He's just being willful. Thomas was right, I've mollycoddled the boy too much and have given him too much attention of late. He can hear me. He will speak normally again. 'Tis his throat—aye, that's—oh, dear God, oh, please don't let him be deaf.* She started to cry. "Poor little lad, poor little baby." She ran back to the nursery and found him huddled in the corner with Anne trying to soothe him.

Rose bent down to pick him up but he pulled away from her. She sent Anne back to her chamber to retrieve the kitten. Rose took the kitten when Anne returned and gently placed it in front of Derry. "There, there, my dearling." He gave her a reproachful look, sniffled and began to pet the kitty. She sat down beside him and stroked his black curls. "Forgive Mama, my dearling, forgive her for being so angry. Mama loves her boy, Mama—" Her voice died out as she realized that he couldn't hear a word she was saying.

Chapter Eleven

ROSE PACED THE parlor floor nervously and hummed a tune as she tried to block out Derry's frightened cries from the nursery. *'Tis for his own welfare—he'll thank me later—oh, what is he doing to him? He is the most skilled physician in London—another cry—oh, my poor baby!* She ran out into the courtyard heedless of the cold winter rain. At least she no longer heard his cries as she walked up the drive and back again.

As she returned to the courtyard, she heard the sound of hoofbeats behind her. She turned and saw Thomas.

"Rose, Rose!" he called to her. "I am joyed that you were keeping watch for me, but to wait in the rain without your cape!" He dismounted and held out his arms to her.

"So you've finally returned," she said crisply and walked quickly toward the door.

"Dearling, what is it?" he called to her.

But she ignored him and marched inside, heedless of the mud she tracked in and the water dripping from her gown. She was standing in front of the parlor fire when Thomas entered.

"Is this a fit greeting for a man returning from abroad?" he asked. "You cannot know what haste I made to arrive before the Christmas season. I had to sail on a—is that Derry crying? Is he ill?"

"Derry is deaf." Rose said and turned around to face Thomas. "I blame myself and you. Basing died in Norwich. I had to leave my son here with servants and journey there to transact your cursed business. If I had not returned when I did, he would surely have perished from fever. Listen to his screams. He fears the physician who's examining him. 'Tis the fifth one I've sent for. Mayhap this one will know a cure, something to bring him out of his frightening world of silence."

"My dear, I am so sorry to hear of the child's affliction." He tried to embrace her but she pushed him away.

"Leave me be. I've had to bear this sorrow alone for weeks; I need no comforting now. I should have married a simple villager. Then at least I would never have to leave my child to do my husband's work."

Thomas stepped back and looked at Rose in shocked silence and then said softly. "You're overwrought with grief; you don't mean those harsh words. Come and sit down, my love." She began sobbing and allowed him to lead her over to a bench. She leaned against his shoulder and wept with anger and frustration.

"Ahem." The physician was poised on the bottom stair. His peaked cap and flowing black robe gave him the appearance of a blackbird perched on a branch.

Rose hastily dried her eyes and asked, "What is your opinion, sir. Can my son be cured?" The physician walked toward them with slow, dignified steps and made a courtly bow. "Oh, forgive me," said Rose. "Physician Woodrofe, this is my husband, Thomas Stratton."

"Your servant, sir," murmured the doctor. "As to my diagnosis," he paused and coughed. "Might I have some refreshment? My throat is still parched from the long journey."

Cider was brought and Woodrofe began speaking, gesturing like a conjurer. "I fear 'tis as I told your servant when he came to fetch me. The fever must have closed up the organs of hearing. It happens once in a great while. I fear your son is permanently deafened."

"But he must have some little hearing left. Oft I have observed him turn around when there is a loud sound behind him."

"Nay, madam, the child but felt the vibrations in the air. Just as if I were to stamp my foot on this wooden floor, you would feel it somewhat through your own foot. Nay, he cannot hear at all."

"Then you can do nothing for him?" asked Thomas.

"Alas, I cannot." Woodrofe looked at Rose and his voice softened. "You can only beg God for mercy."

Rose persisted. "But, sir, you are the greatest physician in London." At this Woodrofe seem to puff up like a preening bird. "Surely you must know some remedy we could try. Have you never cured deafness?"

"Indeed I have, but 'twas of a different sort, the kind which begins with an abcess of the ear. The discharge can ofttimes be treated with adder's oil so that the hearing is restored. But from what you've told me, your son had no symptom but fever. Yea, I fear this is an irrevocable affliction." Rose began to weep and Woodrofe held up his hand and with a sigh said, "Stay, madam, stay your sorrow. Mayhap I do have one remedy that might avail. 'Tis an ancient and carefully guarded mixture."

Rose grabbed his sleeve. "Tell us, please, and we shall pay you handsomely."

Woodrofe pulled his ermine trimmed robe about him. "My dear madam, I do not sell false hope to anyone, but if you insist, I will give your servants instructions for concocting this special poultice."

"Will it pain the child?" asked Rose.

"Nay, 'tis a soothing but somewhat odoriferous remedy. I would not prescribe a harsh treatment. By the looks of it, your son has suffered enough from the ministrations of unskilled physicians or other quacksalvers."

Rose went up to the nursery while Thomas paid Woodrofe and called in the cook to receive instructions for making the poultice. When he joined Rose she had Derry on her lap. Big tears were rolling down the little boy's flushed cheeks as Rose removed his nightshirt to dress him. There were large red welts on his chest.

"What in heaven's name are those marks on Derry?" asked Thomas.

"Oh, those," Rose said as she quickly pulled Derry's shirt down over his head. "The last physician who examined Derry recommended cupping to remove the evil humor that he claimed was causing the deafness. When I protested, he decided the blistering would do as well. He strapped a poultice to Derry's chest that contained powdered blister beetle. There really wasn't much blood lost that way."

"Woodrofe was right," muttered Thomas. "The boy has been treated by quacks."

The cook was standing in the doorway. "Pardon me, sir," she addressed Thomas. "I can obtain the juice of wormwood and the black wool for Master Derry's poultice, but how am I to acquire the gall of a bull?"

"Gall of a bull?" Thomas shook his head. "Let it alone, Rose. These futile remedies will do more harm than good."

"Oh, please," Rose begged him. "Allow this one last cure."

"Very well. It is the slaughtering time. I'll have Humfrey slay the old bull for its gall, but if this cure fails, you must accept the child's fate."

Rose pretended she hadn't heard his last statement and was rocking Derry back and forth in her arms, humming a lullaby she knew he couldn't hear.

That evening as Rose and Thomas sat by the fire in the parlor, Anne came in bearing a bowl at arm's length. With her other hand she covered her nose with a handkerchief. "Here's the concoction, madam. Cook says I'm to dip the black wool in it and place the wool in Derry's ears overnight. Shall I fetch Sybil to help me hold him?"

"Nay," said Rose. "I'll help you."

"But can you not—" Thomas began and then sighed. "Never mind. Go and tend to the lad. I'll sit here alone."

Anne and Rose struggled for the next hour to keep the saturated wool in Derry's ears, but he squirmed and kicked until there were stains of the horrible smelling brew all over his nightclothes and bed linen. At last Rose gave up and decided to let him fall asleep first and then apply the saturated wool. She sent Anne downstairs with the soiled linen and was lying alongside Derry on his bed when Thomas tiptoed in. "Come to bed, my dearling," he whispered. "I've missed you so these past weeks. See, the lad's asleep. I do so crave your presence."

Rose shook her head. "I have not been able to place the remedy in his ears yet. I must wait until he falls into a deeper sleep. I'll come to bed in the space of an hour."

"Let his nurse attend to that."

Rose didn't reply, but began stroking Derry's back. When she looked up Thomas was gone. After a while she was able to place the wool in the sleeping child's ears, and she fell asleep holding it in place.

She awoke at dawn and removed the wool and bathed Derry's head and neck where the evil-smelling potion had run down. Then she took a deep breath and put her face up to Derry's and said, "Derry, my dearling, can you hear Mama?" He smiled and reached out to her. "Oh, he's healed, he's healed!" she cried and carried him into her own bedchamber. Thomas was dressing as she ran up to him.

"He can hear! His ears are opened. Look!" She pulled Derry's face toward her own and spoke softly to him and he smiled again. Thomas was not convinced.

"Put the lad on the bed and then stand behind him and speak," he ordered. With his back to her, Derry didn't turn around when she called, although she almost shouted.

Thomas turned Derry around to face him, smiled and said, "How's the fine lad today? Shall we go and eat some snakes?" Derry smiled and jumped into his arms. "See, Rose, Derry's merely responding to gentle kindly gestures and the expression on my face. I watched you at suppertime. You are so concerned with his affliction that you fail to speak to your son directly or even show him a pleasant countenance."

"But he cannot hear me."

"He can still see. He's a bright boy. He can tell by your expressions whether you are pleased or angry. Why, I had a dog once that could read my every—"

"Stay! Stay!" she shouted. "Now you are comparing him to an animal."

"I didn't mean—I was merely trying to show you that instead of wasting time seeking a cure, you should be trying to help him communicate in some way, help him accept his fate." He put his arm around her. "Let's go riding. The air will do you good and we can talk about it."

She shrugged away his arm. "There's nothing more to talk about. He will hear again, I know it. After all, it's only been a few weeks since his fever." She picked Derry up. "I must get you dressed, my little man." She left the room.

That night in bed Thomas tried to take Rose in his arms but again she turned away. Rose could sense he was glaring at her in the darkness. Then he turned away from her and yanked the coverlet over his shoulders. *He has a right to be angry*, she thought. *But I cannot give in to his embraces. How can I enjoy his love when my sweet little son is in such misery. Oh, Lord, why? why? Derry is just beginning his life. Why did you allow this affliction? Is it enough that his father died a martyr's death? Why must our son be afflicted? What evil has he done, this dear sweet innocent child? Is it me that you are punishing? Mayhap you desired me to stay a widow? Is that it? Oh, God, if you can't or won't heal him, then why didn't you let him die at birth like my other babes? Oh, forgive me, I didn't mean that. But if he must have an affliction, why could it not have been lameness or even blindness? Then at least he could speak and hear. I could tell him of his true father. Oh, Derick, at least you were spared knowing what would befall your son.*

This is all foolish prattle, she told herself. *He will be healed, he will, he will.*

For the next week Rose and Thomas stepped carefully around each other's emotions, making polite talk as if they were strangers. *We are like two figures on a great clock*, Rose thought grimly. *When I come in, he goes out; when he comes in, I go out. If we by chance come near each other, we quickly twirl away.* She no longer pretended to be preoccupied with Derry at bedtime, but often sat up until the middle of the night and slipped into bed when she thought Thomas was sound asleep.

Rose watched helplessly as Derry began to throw tantrums more and more frequently. He would try to talk, to ask for something, and if Anne or Rose were not quick to comprehend his sounds and gestures, he would kick or hit them and throw things. Rose would let him take his anger out on her, but Anne would not. "Here, you little scoundrel," she would say, pinning his arms to his sides, "you cannot behave like that." Then she would patiently try to interpret his needs. But each time Rose failed to understand Derry, she withdrew a little more until she let Anne deal with him most of the day. Once Thomas tried to discipline Derry at supper, but Rose angrily lashed out at him. "Leave him alone! He's not your child!" she snapped. She regretted the words instantly but couldn't seem to help herself. That night she snuggled up to Thomas and didn't turn away as he begin kissing her, but suddenly she sat up. "What was that noise?"

"Nothing," he murmured, "an owl, mayhap. Lie down, my whiting."

"Nay, there it is again. 'Tis Derry having another of his nightmares." She reached for her shawl.

"But Anne is sleeping beside him," Thomas said.

"Ofttimes she doesn't stir when he cries. I'll just go and see." When she returned to the chamber, Thomas was asleep, or at least seemed to be.

Rose awoke the next morning and found Thomas packing his traveling chest. "What is it?" she asked him. "Why are you packing?"

"I'm returning to London. You don't need me here."

"But 'tis only three days until Christmas."

"Is it? Then where is the holly and the carols? Where are the preparations for feasting? This is naught but a house of mourning, and I fear I only add to your misery."

Rose took his hand. "Oh, Thomas, stay, at least for Christmas Day. I'll try to behave as a proper wife, truly I will."

Rose gave instructions to Bess to prepare for a proper Christmas feast for all the household, and put Anne in charge of decking the hall. Then she and Thomas rode into Bury to purchase toys for Derry and gifts for all the household servants. On Christmas Day a huge yule log glowed on the hearth and the serving table groaned under goose, mutton, pork pies, fried smelts, cream mottle, apple tarts and marchpane. All the servants were brought in for a toast, and for a few hours Rose was happy and contented. Anne went caroling with the servants. Thomas insisted Rose and Derry accompany him for a short trip to the stable. Rose gasped with pleasure when she saw a beautiful rust-colored mare with a ribbon wrapped around her neck. "For you, my dearling," he whispered, and gently kissed her on the cheek. Back in the house, Rose and Thomas sat before the fire while Derry played on the floor with his new wooden blocks. He was carefully constructing a tower.

"Look at that," Rose cheerfully exclaimed. "What a clever lad."

She knelt down by Derry and touched him to get his attention and then pointed to the blocks and smiled and applauded. Derry grinned and picked up another block to place on the tower. Suddenly a pained expression came over his face and he clapped his hands over his ears and began moaning. "What is it?" Rose cried. "Are you hurting?" Derry stood up and, still holding his ears, darted about the room whining in high pitched tones. "Oh, Thomas, help me," cried Rose. "We must do something!"

Thomas ran to the boy and tried to pick him up but Derry struggled and kicked and, still whining, ran toward the front door. When he couldn't open it, he leaned against it and hit his head again and again against the door until Thomas picked him up and carried him to his room. Rose watched helplessly while Thomas paced back and forth with Derry straining in his arms until the exhausted child went limp and fell asleep. Thomas laid Derry on his bed and Rose covered the sleeping child and then sat at the foot of his bed and cried silently.

Thomas sat down beside her. "I sorrow for Derry but I sorrow for you, too. Come down to London with me for a while. Leave the lad in Anne's care. You must get some rest from this sad occurrence. Mayhap we can find someone skilled in attending deafened children. Come down with me for a fortnight, at least."

"I cannot—I will not leave him in such torment," she replied.

"Then we'll bring him with us. But you need a change."

She shook her head. "Thomas, I keep remembering a happening of my childhood, when I still lived with my parents in London. A deaf and dumb man lived on Ave Mary Lane. Day after day he would sit outside in the sun, doing nothing but weaving woolen squares on a small handloom. He was sitting by the well at the end of the lane one day when my mother and I went to draw water. He came toward me holding out a withered strawflower, all the while making some pitiful growling sounds. 'Get away from my daughter, you idiot!' screamed my mother and she hit him with her water bucket. Then his own ancient mother rushed up and took him by the hand to lead him into their house. 'He's just trying to be friendly,' his mother said softly. 'Please allow him to give your little girl the flower?' 'Get that monster out of our sight or I shall call the constable and have him put away,' my mother threatened. I still remember the hurt in the woman's eyes and the confused expression on the afflicted man's face. The poor deaf man was never allowed out of his house again." Rose looked at Thomas. "Do you suppose I am being punished now for my mother's unkindness?"

"Rose, your grief has muddled your thinking. How could you even suggest that God would punish you for your mother's deeds? He loves you and He loves Derry."

"Then why, Thomas? Why?"

"I don't know, dear. I simply don't know, but I do know you and the child must go on living. Won't you come to London? You could visit Joan Denley. Have you written her about Derry's affliction?"

"Nay, I—oh, Thomas, how could I have forgotten?" She ran to her bedchamber and rummaged through the portable writing desk until she found Joan's letter which had lain there since Rose's return from Norwich. She sat down on the clothes chest and broke open the letter's wax seal.

Rose:

This is the last you shall hear from me. I know when I am not wanted. I travel the boggy wagon tracks of Essex and Suffolk to surprise little Derry on his birthday. The muck and mire hinders my journey so that I arrive two days late to find you have gone and I am not allowed visit with Derry.

I am amazed at your conduct. How could you leave that dear little lad with such surly servants while you ride off to Norwich? Had I such a precious treasure I would never leave his side for all the goods those Norwich cloth merchants possess. I never left my own son, although now that he's grown, he can't waste time visiting his mother.

The country bumpkins that serve you would only allow me a glimpse of Derry and even now they stand guard while I pen this letter. The idiots fear I might have brought evil vapors from London. Evil vapors indeed. The evil here is that a mother has deserted her child and that one who loves him as her own grandchild cannot even give him a farewell kiss. I'll say no more. You have broken my heart.

Joan

The words on the page became a blur as Rose's eyes filled with tears. Thomas entered the room.

"What is it?" he asked. She handed him the letter and continued to weep as he read it. When he had finished, he angrily crumpled the letter in his hand and threw it to the floor. "That meddlesome woman! She had no right to say those things. You did what you thought was right."

Rose buried her face in her hands. "Nay, she speaks truly. I'm a terrible mother. I should have perished in the fires with the other prisoners. Then Joan could have raised Derry properly."

"Properly? Didn't you read what she wrote? Her own son never comes to see her. She had no right to accuse you. Why, when I return to London I'll tell her to her face what I think of her!"

"Nay, Thomas. She means well. She truly loves Derry and me and I owe her so much. It is I who am to blame. I never took Derry to visit her as I had promised. I never even thought to invite her here for his birthday. I try to do good, but I must be evil. Through my neglect my son is deaf and I've lost a true friend."

"Rose, dearling, don't speak thus." He took out his handkerchief and began to gently wipe away her tears. She turned her face away but he kept his arm around her. "I promise I won't berate Joan, but come down to London with me. I need you, my whiting."

She pulled away from him. "I cannot leave Derry. I will never leave him again. You'd best keep away from me, Thomas. I am a destroyer. Who knows what harm may befall you?"

He looked down into her face for a long time, but she pressed her lips into a tight line and met his sad expression with as hard a look as she could muster.

"Very well," he murmured. "I'll journey to London alone."

Chapter Twelve

THOMAS LEFT FOR London the next day, promising to return to the manor in a few weeks. When he failed to arrive, Rose felt neither disappointment nor anger. He sent several letters but she merely glanced through the apologies and accounts of successful business dealings. She well knew the true reason that kept him away: his own inability to relieve Derry's condition. She even acknowledged that she herself was retreating in her own way, withdrawing into her own mind which seemed to become more and more distant from her feelings and her body. She was eating, sleeping, even talking only when absolutely necessary, but she had withdrawn from real life. She allowed Sybil to take charge of the household and wasn't even disturbed by the murmurings of the cook and the maidservants. She put Derry's care entirely in Anne's hands and walked calmly past both temper tantrums and Derry's silent pleas for her attention.

Rose knew, too, in her detached, emotionless mind, that she was behaving in just the same way as she had following Derick's death at the stake. *And why shouldn't I*, she thought. *My son, the normal, whole child begotten of my beloved Derick, lives no more. The child that might have become a minister, or a writer of Christian truth, or a charitable merchant, is dead. In his place there is a confused, tormented little prisoner of silence*. Why should she not mourn? But her mourning was silent and cold and solitary.

Through the first months of the new year she fell into a routine. Each day she would walk or ride Brownie, the horse Thomas had given her, great distances alone until she was physically exhausted.

Then, in the evening, she would sit and stare into the parlor hearth fire until everyone else had retired. She noticed the servants' whispered conferences and the puzzled looks on the farmhands' faces, but she kept to her routine. She felt that if she should stray from it, she would go raving mad. When Thomas's letters showed concern, she forced herself to scribble a few lines back, assuring him that she and Derry were fine. She feared if she did not, he would ride up from London and disturb the order of her days.

Gradually, as a boat drifts toward the shoreline, Rose felt herself drifting back to reality. Her detached thoughts reached solid ground with a "thud" one morning in March when she passed by the entrance to the kitchen and was hit in the face by a piece of pastry dough.

"Oh, mistress, forgive me!" cried the cook. Sybil, with a furious look on her face, brushed by Rose as she hurried outside.

Bess bustled up to Rose and began cleaning the dough from her hair. "I don't know what came over me," she was saying. "I was arguing with Sybil and something she said made me see red and I was kneading dough at the time and I—"

Rose began laughing and kept at it until there were tears in her eyes and she had to lean against the kitchen table while she caught her breath. Bess fetched her a mug of cider, and Rose sat down and dried her eyes on a dish towel.

"If I lose my position for this, 'tis worth it, madam, just to hear your laughter again."

"I wouldn't dismiss you, Bess, but you and Sybil must stop this fighting. What was it about this time?"

Bess blushed. "Well, mayhap I was mocking her overmuch. But she said my pottage tasted like sheep dip and I said how did she know, an old spinster with no taste at all—love struck over Tom, the pride of the village drunkards, who only takes his nose out of the ale pot long enough to spit on the floor."

" 'Tis natural to desire to wed."

"True, but why doesn't she seek a decent man in a decent way? Trying to buy love potions, she was."

Suddenly Rose felt an overwhelming desire to hold Derry, something she hadn't done in many weeks. She scurried off to search and found him with Anne in the walled garden. It was still bare except for a few daisies and some ground ivy beginning to spread its greenery across one corner of the garden. Derry was busily constructing a farm with his cast iron horses and cows. Anne was sitting on a stone bench nearby and stood up when Rose approached.

"Good day, madam," Anne said and watched Rose warily. *Have I been behaving so strangely that she is frightened of me?* wondered Rose.

"Dear Anne, I've placed a heavy burden on you these last months," apologized Rose. "But I—I'm feeling better now and will help you more." She sat down by Derry and he looked up at her with such an angelic smile that Rose was overwhelmed with remorse for ignoring him so long. "Oh, my baby, my dear baby," she cried and pulled him onto her lap. Derry sat quietly in her lap and allowed her to rock him back and forth in her arms as she sobbed. "Mama won't neglect you anymore." She held him and kissed him until he began to squirm out of her grasp. "All right, my little wiggleworm, enough affection. Let us do something little boys enjoy. Anne, fetch two hand spades. Derry and I are going to plant some flowers."

As she and Derry began to dig side by side in the soft, warm earth, Rose felt that her heart was becoming soft once again too. She silently talked to God in a way she hadn't been able to for a long while.

My Father in Heaven, forgive me for indulging in self-pity, and allowing myself to grow far away from you. I know you've been near me all this time, only I was too stubborn to reach out to you in faith. Help me to be the wife and mother you want me to be. I will try to accept your will for Derry. And thank you for your well of grace and mercy that never runs dry . . .

Rose continued praying in this manner as she and Derry planted the flowers. He looked up into her face at one point, gaping in wonder at the glowing look of peace he hadn't seen before. He smiled and patted her arm.

"Oh, Derry!" she said and hugged him again.

An hour later she was still on her knees turning up soil when she saw Thomas and a stranger enter the garden. Her heart took a turn at the sight of Thomas and she would have run to him if the gangly young man had not been present. She arose and hastily brushed the dirt from her gown. "My little gardeners," said Thomas, smiling at her. "Your letter—I was afraid you were ill or—"

"I'm fine, now," she said and reached up to smooth a wisp of hair. Thomas caught her hand and kissed it. "Forgive me for staying away so long."

"There's nothing to forgive. I—Derry—there's nothing to fear." The little boy had been digging furiously and hadn't seen the two men approach. Now when he looked up and saw the stranger, he grabbed Rose's skirt and was trying to pull her away.

"If I frighten the lad, I could wait in the courtyard," the young man volunteered. He had removed his cap and was smoothing down his straw-colored hair.

"Nay, Robert. Rose, this is Robert Gilbert. I first met this young fellow when I traveled to Geneva during our time of exile. He was training for the ministry then, and he's straining for a ministry now."

Robert laughed so pleasantly at this gentle gibe that Rose took an instant liking to him. "Aye, 'tis true. I am straining. I have not been appointed to any parish yet. I'll take any position at this point, even chaplain to a cloth merchant."

Rose looked questioningly at Thomas, and he grinned. "Robert jests. He's on his way to visit relatives in Lynn, and I invited him to spend a few days with us. Having our own chaplain might be a wise move, however. The minister in Goodthorpe is resentful that we do not attend his services. So far Her Majesty has been lenient to the gentry, but we may soon be required to attend the authorized church, I fear."

"Oh, Thomas, is it starting again? Will we be persecuted for not worshiping as the Queen directs?"

"I pray not so, madam," Robert said with spirit. "England will never allow the burning of its citizens again, shield God." At a warning glance from Thomas, the young man turned red and said, "Forgive me, madam, Thomas has told me of your first husband's martyrdom and I have no wish to bring you grievous memories."

There was an awkward silence and then Thomas clapped Robert on the shoulder. "Well, Rose, now you see one reason this young man has been denied a parish thus far. He cannot bridle his tongue. The officials fear his theology since he sat at the feet of the Calvinists.

So I brought him home to give him chance to air his ideas to a friendly audience. If he is a poor preacher, he can always help with the farmwork. What say you, Robert, could you spread manure?"

"Aye, is that not what we preachers are oft accused of doing? Oh, my pardon, Mistress Stratton!"

Robert was so obviously distressed that she choked back a laugh and merely nodded her head. She caught Thomas's approving eye.

Robert knelt down and completely won Derry over when he made horseriding gestures and soon Anne and Derry were taking the young minister to the stables to show him Derry's pony.

"Robert's a sound lad," Thomas said as he watched him leave, "but he's lived too monastic a life. His views are not always grounded in reality. I thought it would do him good to stay with a Christian family. You don't mind, do you?"

"Nay, he seems to have made friends with Derry and he is a jolly fellow. 'Tis good to laugh again."

Thomas looked worried as he took her hand and said, "My dear, I have some—" he paused and searched her eyes—"Nay, it can wait. Come let's join the others." Rose was curious, but didn't want to press him. Like Thomas, she had no desire to spoil this pleasant moment.

After supper Robert entertained them with stories of his student days in Geneva. He had a charming way of laughing at himself. Anne lingered, obviously smitten by the young minister, until Rose had to gently remind her that it was past Derry's bedtime. Along with his humor, Robert's apparent zeal attracted Rose. He had such an intense, confident manner when he spoke of spiritual matters. When Thomas offered to take Robert upstairs to see the small house chapel, Rose said, "You're tired from your journey. Stay by the fire and I'll show Robert the chapel."

"Am I a graybeard too feeble to totter up the stairs?" Thomas protested mildly and then settled more comfortably in his chair.

"So you are," answered Robert. "When we return I shall carry you to your chamber."

In the chapel Rose said, "As you see, 'tis quite small, with just room for our family and the household servants. They prefer, however, to worship in the Goodthorpe church as their families have done for generations."

"I wonder that people can be so blind," stated Robert. "It matters little to them if rituals and traditions are still observed as in former times. They are told to go to a church and to the church they go. Poor blind villagers."

"Not all villagers are blind," Rose retorted. "One named Mallorie died for his faith on the village green, leaving a widow and six children. My Derick was a villager also."

"Again my unbridled tongue. Forgive me, 'tis my besetting sin, I fear."

She ignored his apology and asked, "Robert, Thomas must have told you how Derry lost his hearing. What have your studies in the Scriptures taught you about healing?"

The young minister rubbed his jaw thoughtfully. "I must confess, I have not given much time to searching out Christ's teaching on the subject, but I would say—" he paced about the little chapel with his hands behind his back. "I would say—well, let us take an instance of healing. If you'll recall the healing of the woman with an issue of—with an affliction she had endured for some time. Now she was not afflicted from birth but stricken later on, so the situation would be similar. What did she do to be healed? She touched the hem of Christ's garment, and," his tones became that of an orator, "how did she touch the hem? She must have stooped low, knelt on the ground. In other words, she humbled herself. Aye, that is the remedy. I must write that down for use in a sermon."

"Derry is only a small child, and deaf. How can he humble himself more?"

"You, as his mother, must do it for him. Confess to all those you've wronged; be meekly obedient to your husband and I think, nay, I know that the child will be healed."

"Oh, if that would be true! Can you find your way back to the parlor, Robert? I wish to pray alone for a space."

"Of course, madam."

Later when she retired Rose spoke excitedly to Thomas, "My dear, I think I have been shown the key to Derry's healing. I have been too contrary and prideful. I asked God's forgiveness for my sins but I still must—" she fell down on her knees before him. "Oh, I've harmed you most of all. Forgive me for being a rebellious and froward wife, for shunning your company in bed, for neglecting your welfare and if there are any other ways I've grieved you, tell me and I'll most humbly repent." She gazed up at him pleadingly.

Thomas looked embarrassed, "Come, my dear. There's no need—" he began.

"And I must journey to London to ask Joan's forgiveness. I've wronged a true friend by not visiting her or answering her last letter."

"Rose, Rose, I must tell you—" He helped her up and looked distressed as he said, "The sorrowful news I was going to relate, 'tis about Joan Denley. She's dead. She died the day before yesterday."

"But how—?" In a daze Rose sat on the bed. Thomas sat down beside her and put his arm around her. "I put aside my past dislike of Joan Denley because I thought it would do you good to have your old friend come to visit. So I went to see her. The shop on London Bridge was locked up but I kept knocking on the door until a servant opened it for me. She recognized me and showed me up to Joan's bedchamber. In spite of a generous sprinkling of herbs about the room, the air was hot and thick and smelled of death. I would never have recognized Joan, she was—" he took Rose's hand. "I fear I distress you too much."

"Nay, go on. I want to know," Rose assured him as she tightly clutched his hand.

"Her skin had turned saffron yellow and her face was swollen beyond recognition. Propped up on a mountain of pillows and bolsters, she yet gasped for air. Jack, her manservant, stood on one side of the bed and a maidservant on the other. Joan would gasp for air and then frantically grip their hands and struggle to rise. They would help her up until she was sitting upright in her effort to take air into her lungs. Then she would fall back upon the pillows and lie for a few moments in a stupor, and once again strain to breathe. I shall never forget the agonizing look in her eyes."

"Could she speak at all?" Rose asked as tears rolled down her cheeks.

"Nay, it was as if she were drowning. She recognized me, I think, and tried to speak, but made just a gurgling sound from deep in her throat. As I stood there, she attempted once more to sit up and then as she fell back, she sighed out her last breath and gave up the ghost."

"Oh, what a wretch I am!" cried Rose. "I should have gone to see her. There will be no one at her burial."

"Her son arrived just as I left. He came from York, I believe."

"Aye. He's a swordsmith there. Joan is—was so proud of him. Oh, Thomas, I am glad you were there at her deathbed, but 'tis I who should have been holding her hand. Did you inquire—did the servants know if she had ever confessed Christ?"

"I asked, but Jack did not know. But she might have confessed to Christ alone dearling, as she lay in her deathbed. Take comfort in that thought."

"How can I? I should have been there to read Scriptures to her and ask her plainly if she would confess that she was a sinner and that Christ had died to save her. I have failed. No wonder the Lord has hidden His face from me." She began sobbing. Thomas stroked her hair and tried to console her.

The next morning she came downstairs with her hair unbound and wearing her plainest gown. She paused to kiss Derry as he was eating porridge in the kitchen with Anne. "Madam, you look ill," said the girl. "Have some cider."

"Nay," said Rose in a faraway voice. "I shall not eat or drink today." Thomas and Robert were already out riding and Rose spent the morning in the chapel. She read the Scriptures and prayed and paced the floor. At noon Thomas came up to call her to dinner.

"I have begun a fast," she told him. "In the night I remembered the Bible account of the boy whose affliction caused him to fall into a fire and harm himself. When the apostles could not heal him, do you remember what our Lord said to them? 'This kind cometh not out but by prayer and fasting.' Don't you see, Thomas? The solution has been there all along, but I have been blind to it. I have not really prayed for Derry's healing unless I have prayed *and* fasted."

Thomas said nothing for a moment. The scent of fresh baked bread wafted up from the kitchen and caused Rose's stomach to growl, but she clutched her sides and remained on her knees. "Very well, my dear," Thomas said and softly shut the door. Rose continued to pray over and over, "Lord, heal my son. Lord, heal my son." The day wore slowly on. She fell asleep praying several times and when evening came, she struggled to her feet. Her head was pounding and she went immediately to bed.

The next morning she again shut the door to the little chapel and spent the day fasting, praying and reading the Scriptures. Several times she heard a little knocking on the door and knew that Derry wanted to see her, but she called out, "I'm doing this for you, dearling," to strengthen her own resolve. When he began crying by the door, she told Anne to take Derry out to ride his pony.

"But 'tis raining, madam," Anne replied. "Derry misses your company. Could you not come out for a bit or let him in there with you?"

"Nay," Rose called. "Please take him downstairs." She picked up the Bible and tried to read again and was sitting on the floor when Thomas and Robert entered.

Robert hesitated, then with a quick glance at Thomas began, "Mistress Stratton, I would be the last to deter anyone from worshiping God, but mayhap you have taken the Scriptures too literally in this instance. God uses our bodies as His dwelling place and we should not harm them either by too much meat or drink or by too little. There is danger in placing confidence in rituals."

"How can you speak thus, Master Gilbert, when you yourself boasted to us that you once fasted a fortnight?"

"Aye, but I had drink—"

"Were you fasting for God to hear on high and heal someone you love?"

"Nay, but—"

"Then do not advise me how to fast." She brushed a hand across her dried and cracked lips. "If you gentlemen will leave me to my prayers." Thomas hustled the younger man out and slammed the door behind them.

The next morning Rose was so weak she couldn't get out of bed. Thomas stormed in with Anne following behind, bearing a tray with some bread and a mug of cider. "I am your husband and I command you to eat and drink," he said. Her lips were so swollen that she couldn't reply, and he put his arm under her shoulders and spoke more gently as he helped her sit up, "Please, my whiting, just a sip of cider." She turned her head away from the mug he held.

"The healing—" she whispered.

"Derry's ears have not been opened. I just called to him. I'm sorry, my dear, but I feel this fasting is in vain. There are times to fast, I agree, but can it be proper to harm yourself and deprive Derry of his mother's company?''

"Whatever it takes," she whispered.

"Well, it is not this. Drink, I say."

She obediently sipped some cider and turned away. "More," he commanded. She drank another sip and then felt nauseous.

"Some water—"

"Of course." Anne fetched some and she drank.

"There, you're going to feel better now. I'll have the cook prepare some broth." Thomas left the room.

Rose fell back on her pillow. *Oh, Father*, she prayed, *if fasting is not the key, what is?* Her glance fell on the tapestry which hung on the wall. It was a picture of three pilgrims on horseback. Each was wearing the shell, symbol of pilgrimages, pinned to his hat. *A pilgrimage. That's it. I must go on a pilgrimage. Did not even King Henry make a pilgrimage to the shrine at Walshingham? Ah, but that was devoted to Mary, the mother of Jesus. I must journey to a place significant to my own spiritual life. Boxton? Should I take Derry to the very spot where his father was burned at the stake?* She shuddered at the thought. She had made one visit there after her release from prison—prison. That was it. She would make a pilgrimage with her son to the place where she had first come to know the Lord. She would take him to Newgate Prison.

Thomas came back into the chamber with a bowl of broth. He was pleased that she ate it with no protest.

"Thomas, when are you returning to London?" she asked.

"Why, I had planned on next Monday. Robert is going to ride with me as far as Newmarket where we would part company. But I could stay here longer if you—"

"Nay, nay," she said impatiently. "You must go then. We will go with you, Derry and I. We must go with you to London."

Chapter Thirteen

ROSE HELD DERRY'S hand tightly as they walked down Cheapside toward Newgate Prison. The London street was crowded with people but she rushed past them, her mind intent upon her destination. She had not told Thomas or Anne what she planned to do. Thomas seemed so pleased that she had accompanied him to the city that she had felt a pang of guilt when she kissed him good-bye as he left their town-house that morning. He had to arrive at Blackwell Hall early to purchase cloths from the Halifax clothiers.

Derry kept tugging at her sleeve and pointing at the sights and making unintelligible sounds. He wanted to stop and look into every shop and stall. As she pulled him along she prayed that he wouldn't have one of his tantrums on the street. She thought it odd that he seemed most curious of the lame and deformed beggars which inhabited every corner. He looked at one white-haired old woman with a terribly twisted body and refused to go any farther. Rose put a coin in the woman's hand and Derry solemnly patted the beggar on the arm. His tender look of concern brought tears to Rose's eyes. *Will he have such a sympathetic heart when people begin to mock and shun him?* she thought. *Shield, God, no one will ever have the opportunity to shame him.*

They had almost reached the prison. She picked Derry up and carried him the rest of the way, keeping her eyes down as she walked so that she didn't actually see the building until she was standing by its gray, stone wall. She hadn't trusted herself to view it from afar. After she and other Protestant prisoners had been released that winter day two years ago, she had carefully avoided the sight of the place. While she had recovered from her long imprisonment, there was no way to avoid sights of others' sufferings; they were everywhere about the city, but it was the sight of Newgate that she dreaded most.

The stench of human excrement wafted up from the barred cell windeyes at street level. Rose took a firmer grip on Derry and resolutely climbed the stairs to the prison entrance.

The doorkeeper squinted at her through his one good eye when he answered her knock. "No visitors," he muttered and then looked her over carefully as if taking note of her fine clothes. "No visitors, no matter how highborn the prisoner. However, I will be happy to show special consideration for any captive, for certain fees." He unconsciously rubbed his hands together in anticipation.

Derry threw his arms around his mother and looked away from the doorkeeper. Rose patted the child gently and said in a quavering voice. "I came not to visit any captive—I wish to visit an empty cell."

The keeper laughed and then grinned broadly, showing the stumps of rotted teeth. "What are you, a sunstruck loony? Go away." He began to close the door.

"Wait!" she cried. "I will pay you handsomely if you allow me to visit an empty cell but for a few moments."

He shook his head wonderingly. " 'Tis a cell in Bedlam you are wanting, but," he paused and eyed her purse, "wait here and if the lord jailer should question why you are standing here, say you are waiting while I bring you the belongings of your brother who perished in prison."

Rose waited for what seemed to be an hour. Derry fidgeted and struggled, trying to get down. At last the doorkeeper came with a torch. "Shh, not a sound. If I am caught, 'twill mean my position." He conducted her down some steps and unlocked a door. Up from the stairs below came the dank stench that made her gag and Derry flail the air with his hands. She held her perfumed handkerchief up to Derry's nose as she carefully followed the keeper down the stone stairway to the open door of the first of three cells. She hesitated at the doorway. On a wooden bench inside, a small candlestick with the stub of a candle flickered. A trencher containing the dried remains of some gray mixture was the only other item in the cell. The keeper lit the candle with his torch and withdrew. "A few moments, no more," he whispered and shut the heavy door. Derry clung to her, his eyes wild with fear. She held him tightly. "Hush, hush, my love," she crooned, and put his head against her throat so that he could feel the vibrations of her soft singing. When he had quieted down she prayed aloud, "Oh, Lord, here we are, if not in the same cell, at least one like to it where I first realized that you had died for me, where I repented of my sins and asked you to save me. Oh, Lord, from that day you have never forsaken me, I know that now. You guarded the child in my womb. On filthy straw like this he was born and yet in your mercy you delivered him from the clutches of the evil jailkeeper's wife. Now behold, Lord, his affliction. How can he serve you and glorify your name if his ears are stopped? Heal him now, I beg you, in Jesus' name." Just then the slight bit of candle melted down into wax and the flame was extinguished. Derry wailed and Rose tried to open the door. It was locked. "Let us out, let us out!" she cried, and pounded the door with her fist. When there was no answer, she stood on tiptoe and glanced out of the small barred opening. She could see nothing but darkness. "Let us out of here," she called again and then saw a glimmer of light appear to the left of her. It grew stronger as the keeper brought his torch down the stairs and looked into the cell. "Aw, gave you a fright, didn't I? Serves you right for attempting such a crazed adventure. Fine ladies like you should stay home and embroider. Pass your purse through these bars and I'll unbolt the door."

"Nay, I shall not," Rose said. "I shall pay you when we are safely outside the prison."

"I could leave you in there overnight. No one would know."

Rose thought quickly. "My husband knows. He is Thomas Stratton, a well-known merchant and I told him I was coming here. If I don't return home soon, he will bring the High Constable to investigate."

At that the keeper unbolted the door and grudgingly escorted her to the exit. She tossed the bag of coins at him and ran down the stairs to the street. Derry was crying and she was trembling from her close call as she hurried toward Thames Street. It wasn't until she reached her own doorstep that she remembered to test Derry's hearing. She set him down and smoothed his clothes and wiped his tear-stained face. "There now, my love." She took several deep breaths and turned him away from her, facing the street. Then she cried excitedly, "Look, over there, your pony!" but he showed no sign of hearing her. Her shoulders slumped in disappointment. She put her hand on the handle of the door just as it was opened by a plump, raven-haired woman. "Rose, dear sister-in-law, was that you shouting like a fishwife?"

"Mirabel?"

"In the flesh. I'll wager you're surprised to see me." She gestured toward Derry who was still facing the street. "And who is that? Why does he keep his back—"

"This is my son, Derry." Rose cut her off and gently turned Derry around and put a protective hand on his shoulder. "Shall we go inside?"

Derry began to cry and Rose carried him into the parlor. Anne was busily entertaining two twin girls. Rose swiftly calculated that they must be about four months older than Derry although they appeared to be half a head taller than he. She resented the fact that they were both chattering away. They both had blond hair like her brother, Robin, but they already had acquired their mother's pouty expression. A smaller raven-haired boy was balancing on the edge of a bench. Thomas stood by the fireplace and greeted Rose with a long-suffering look on his face. "There you are. What have you and Derry been up to? No one seemed to know where you went."

Rose blushed and murmured. "Walking. We were just walking." She looked around. "But where's Robin. Where's my brother?"

"Here I am, Rose."

She turned around and saw her brother entering from the hall. His blond hair had thinned more, making his forehead even higher, but he had the same sweet smile she remembered, although there was a weary dullness to his eyes. She kissed him and he gave her a long hug. "How came you back to England?" she asked. "Thomas told me that you had a fine position in Frankfurt."

"I did," he said, "but Mir—but *we* could not abide the customs of that city and so we journeyed to Antwerp. There we met a business associate of Thomas's and when he learned that I was your brother, the gentleman kindly offered to—"

"To escort us back to London," finished Mirabel.

"Nay, to pay our passage back to London," responded Robin firmly. "To be short, we were destitute. This morning the gentleman escorted us to Blackwell Hall where we found Thomas. Your husband has generously offered to set me up in my own printing establishment here in London and allow us the hospitality of your home until we can find quarters."

Rose looked gratefully at Thomas. He was so kind and generous in using his wealth to help others. She suddenly had a great hunger to be held in his arms. *I love you. I do love you*, she thought as she gazed at him. He must have caught the message in her eyes, for he walked over to her and laid his hand on her shoulder, something he rarely did before others. "After dinner we can look for a shop to lease, Robin, while our wives get reacquainted." He must have felt Rose flinch at that suggestion, for he quickly added, "and we must find you a suitable dwelling for your family. I know you will wish your own quarters as soon as possible."

The twin girls walked up to Derry, but he hid behind Rose's skirts. "Say hello to your cousin, girls," Mirabel ordered. When Derry didn't reply to their sing-song greeting, Mirabel said, "What's wrong with you, boy? Cat got your tongue?"

"He's tired," Anne hastily said and took his hand. "Shall I take him to bed, madam?"

"Nay," said Thomas. "You can take him out into the garden with the other children while we have a quiet dinner."

"But—" Rose began.

Thomas drew her closer to him. "They'll be fine. Derry needs to play with other children." But Rose watched anxiously as Anne led the children outdoors.

After dinner when the men left, Rose endured Mirabel's self-pitying account of the last few years. The only incident she could truly sympathize with was the loss of a stillborn child, but Mirabel felt it was a blessing not to have another child to care for. Resentment welled up in Rose, and in spite of her resolve to be kind and forgiving to everyone, she was glad when Anne brought all the children upstairs for naps. Alone with Anne and Derry in the nursery, Rose asked,

"Did he play well with the children?"

"He did with the little boy, madam. They raced about the garden and when Derry gestured that he wanted to play ball, the child understood perfectly. But the little girls, the twins—they turned away from Derry every time he attempted to make friends. They seem to have a cruel streak in them."

Just like their mother, thought Rose, but aloud she said, "The little girls probably are weary from their sea journey. I'm sure my brother's children are really kindhearted."

Alone in her own bedchamber, Rose sat on the bed and buried her face in her hands. The pilgrimage to Newgate Prison had been a failure. She had been so certain that God had wanted her to make it. What had gone wrong? Should she have gone to Boxton first and shown Derry the spot on the green where his father was killed? *Is that it, Lord? Why can't I know clearly? Tell me what you require of me.* She waited for a long time with her head bowed, but she felt nothing, received no message in her mind. A deadening weariness crept over her and she lay down and cried into the pillow.

Supper was an irritating affair. Mirabel seemed jealous of Robin and Rose's conversation and burst in at every occasion. When she went upstairs to attend to her children and came down to find Robin and Rose reminiscing about their father, she promptly started a quarrel with Robin and ran upstairs in tears. With a sigh and a shrug of his shoulders, Robin followed his wife to their chamber and never came back down that evening.

The next day Thomas went to his own books in the counting house on the street level of their house and Mirabel and Robin went out together to hunt for a dwelling. Rose helped Thomas with the books for a while and then felt guilty that Anne should have to care for all the children. She went out into the garden to ask if the girl needed help. Anne was nowhere in sight and Derry was sitting on the ground with a frightened look on his face while the other children pelted him with gravel from the walk. "Freak, freak, cannot speak!" the little girls were chanting. Even the little boy was trying to echo their words and fling pebbles in Derry's direction.

"Stop! Stop! You wicked, wicked children!" Rose shouted. As she grabbed one of the girl's arms and yanked her hand away from the gravel walk, the girl fell to the ground and began crying. The other girl and little boy ran back to the doorway just as Anne came out.

"Where have you been?" Rose screamed. "They were attacking Derry."

"Oh, madam, I didn't know—I just went to the kitchen to fetch these for the children." She held up a plate of hot cross buns. "I— forgive me."

Rose picked up Derry and ignored the crying twin still seated on the ground. " 'Tis not your fault," she said as she carried Derry to the door. " 'Tis mine for allowing him to be exposed to them."

Anne helped the twin up and took her by the hand. "The children don't know right from wrong yet."

"They called my son a freak and pelted him with stones. A freak! They didn't know that word, I'll wager, until their mother taught it to them. She brushed past the other two children as she said, "Take all three of them up to their bedchamber and keep them there until their parents return. I want them out of my sight!"

The counting house was on the opposite side of the house from the garden, so Thomas knew nothing of the scene until he came up to the bedchamber later.

"Rose, the maidservant says you're not coming down to dinner. Robin and Maribel are waiting and—Rose, dearling, what are you doing?"

"What does it look like? I'm packing. I was wrong to bring Derry to the city. I thought—I imagined, I suppose, that God wanted me to come, but now I see it was wrong. We shall leave for the manor tomorrow." She turned around to face him and there were two bright red spots on her cheeks. "I'll not stand by and see my child mocked and injured by cruel children." She broke down and told him what had happened.

"It must have hurt you deeply," Thomas said, "but you needn't leave. I'll find Robin and his family other accommodations, an inn perhaps. Please don't leave so soon. I want to be with you as much as possible. I must go on another journey in a week's time, to Spain. I fear our relations with that country are becoming more strained as the Queen keeps fending off Philip's proposals of marriage. I have just begun shipping them Suffolk cloths and importing skins and chamois leather. I need to journey there myself to secure a deal in wheat."

Her voice sounded bitter as she said, "Aye, Thomas, I wondered when you would leave again. I might as well be a nun, for all the time my husband spends at home with me." A strange look came over her face. "Is that it? Have I hit upon the reason for Derry's affliction? Mayhap the Lord was displeased that we wed, Thomas."

"Stop! Stop this nonsense!" He grabbed her by the shoulders and shook her. She was startled by his fierce expression.

"And will you beat me as well?" she asked softly.

He relaxed his grip on her. "If I thought it would end this futile seeking after cures, I would. Be truthful. Did you come to London to find another physician?"

"Nay," she replied and avoided his eyes. This was not the time to tell him of her pilgrimage.

"Derry is deaf. He will always be deaf, and you and I and the child must go on living."

She pulled away from him. "What a marvelous life he lives," she mumbled sarcastically.

"A better life than if we had not wed, I'll wager. At least he will never have to beg for a living. Think on this. For some unfathomable reason, which only God knows, Derry was stricken with deafness, but in His mercy God brought us together so that Derry might have all the comfort and care my wealth could give him."

"Rich or poor, he'll never be like other men. Oh, Thomas! I had such great plans for his life. I thought God could use him mightily, that he would be all his father never had a chance to be."

"I know, my dearling, I know." He embraced her as he continued. "God still has a purpose in his life. He hasn't deserted you or your son, and I'll not desert you either. I'll try not to let my business rule my life. I could send someone to Spain in my place—a new assistant mayhap—although after the fiasco with Edmund in Antwerp—ah well, that is a matter I can work out. The important fact is that I must bear the burden with you and help you to accept Derry's fate."

Rose set her jaw, thinking, *Not yet, not yet. I won't accept it until I've tried everything in heaven and earth*. Aloud, she said, "Go on with your journey to Spain, Thomas. Merchanting is your gift and you must use it. Derry and I will await your return at Grendal Hall." He studied her face a moment and then took his arms from around her and muttered, "As you wish."

That evening Rose forced herself to dine with the others for Robin's sake. "I heard you were unwell this morning," said Robin. "Was it a headache?"

"Probably indigestion from venting her spleen on our chi—" A sharp look from Robin stopped Mirabel. Rose was cheered to see that Robin seemed to have more control over his selfish wife nowadays. He might have warned her that if she didn't watch her tongue, they would be out on their ears. At any rate, Rose was pleased that Mirabel kept her mouth shut for the rest of the supper. She opened it only to stuff capons, bread and a host of herbs into it. Rose waited until Mirabel had gone upstairs, and then she and Robin strolled into the garden to say farewell.

"It seems we are always parting," Robin said.

"I know, but I must return to the manor. Derry needs to live a quiet life." She took her brother's arm. "At least now we won't be separated by water. I know your printing business will succeed. You're such a fine printer. Father would have been proud."

"He wouldn't have been proud of the way my children treated Derry. I teach them to be kind but—"

Rose knew what he left unspoken. Mirabel's sharp tongue could easily undo all his patient instruction. In a way he was following the pattern of their father who was so gentle compared to their demanding, strident mother.

"Don't blame yourself. Derry is—different and children can be so cruel. We will both be more comfortable back on the estate."

"I shall be praying for your son and someday, mayhap, I can visit Grendal Manor. *Alone.*" They both smiled and she kissed him on the cheek.

Chapter Fourteen

ANNE WAS MUCH disappointed that they wouldn't be staying in London. Rose soothed her by allowing her to buy gifts for her family and agreeing to drop her off at their cottage for a week's visit. She also wanted to make arrangements with Widow Malorie to send some of the knitted goods from their widows' guild up to Yarmouth Fair which was held Easter week. She had neglected her business venture also during the months since Derry lost his hearing.

Widow Malorie rushed out to greet them as they rode up.

"Anne, I've missed you so. Good-day, Mistress Stratton. Is something amiss?"

"Nay," Rose assured her. "Anne is a wonderful nurse. She craved to visit you, and so I've brought her to stay a week."

"Mother, I've been to London," Anne bubbled excitedly.

"How wondrous!" her mother exclaimed. "Now you'll have time to tell us all about it." Widow Malorie frowned as she looked at Derry. "How is the lad? I've heard of his affliction. I sorrow for him and for you, my dear."

The sympathy in her voice caused Rose to fight back tears. Derry began gesturing that he wanted to get down and play with the children who had run up to greet them. The widow took her children aside and said, "Derry can't hear anymore, so you boys be kind to him and show him the fort you've made by the oak. The widow reached up for Derry and after a moment's hesitation, Rose handed him down and then dismounted herself. The two boys solemnly took Derry by the hand and walked off to play.

121

"Come into the cottage, my dear, and we'll have some fresh cider." The widow shooed her other children out into the garden. Anne was already regaling her twelve-year-old sister with descriptions of London sights. Rose sat at the trestle table with the widow and relaxed. The cottage reminded her of her home in Boxton. In spite of herself Rose was soon telling the widow all she had done to seek for a cure for Derry.

"Margaret, you're a mother and believer. Can you see what more I can do?" Rose concluded. "Why do you suppose God hasn't answered my prayers? I know He is able to heal."

Margaret sighed. "I know not, though I wish I did. My own son Richard, the one who lost his life in a farming accident, was born with one weak limb. I counted it a miracle the day he learned to walk. By sixteen, he could work as hard as anyone and he hardly limped at all. And yet he died. All because he had scratched his hands on stinking mayweed as he was helping with the harvest. It caused the poison in his blood. He was in the prime of youth. I stopped asking 'why' after a season and just thanked the Lord He had given him to me for those sixteen years. People told me when he died that at least I had more children to console me. But each one is precious in my sight, and I know that is how God feels about each one of us. I know by God's very nature that He loved my Richard far more than I ever could and so I just rest on that."

"I wish I could rest," Rose said wistfully. "I just don't know what to do. If God gives knowledge to physicians, shouldn't we seek them out?"

"Mayhap. I would have sought any cure for Richard, but it happened so fast. Do you think, though, that God truly gives all wisdom to all physicians? Even if I could afford one for my children when they are ill, I would fear to do so. They are but the blind leading the blind in some ways. They bleed, purge and sweat the sick until the cures are worse than the diseases. These things are unnatural. What does a beast of the field do when it is sick? It eats certain grasses or rolls in soothing mud. I believe the Lord has given us herbs and plants and powder from the earth to cure every disease that afflicts man. We just don't have the knowledge to find and use all of the remedies He has provided. Of course I am an ignorant woman who cannot read, but I know some uses of healing herbs and soothing balms. I only wish I knew one to help your son."

"What you say seems very wise. Somewhere there must be an herb that could heal Derry." She stood up. "We must be going if we would reach the manor by dark. I'll send for Anne next week."

Derry was reluctant to leave and that pleased Rose. It showed her he could play happily with children who were kind.

The next morning she asked the cook, "Are there any herbs or plants grown in these parts noted for their medicinal qualities?"

Bess considered. "Just the usual. Eyeseed and paigle, Bear's garlic will soon be growing in the woodlands. Coltsfoot's a pesky weed but 'tis good for the chest. Comfrey leaves. Nothing unusual to my knowledge."

"And are you so great an authority?" Sybil, who had been sweeping nearby, now spoke up.

"Better than you," the cook retorted. "Tell Mistress Stratton how well your love potions worked."

Sybil stalked out in a fury. "Her beloved staggered out of a tavern one night and hasn't been seen since," the cook said loud enough for Sybil to hear.

The next morning Rose heard moans coming from the kitchen. She found Bess by the fireplace, doubled over with pain. "I've been poisoned, poisoned," she groaned. "There was something in my porridge."

"Nonsense," said Rose as she helped her to the bench. "You're the one who cooked it. Besides, we all ate porridge at breakfast and none of us is sick. You've just taken a cramp."

"Nay," the cook insisted, "I fancied I'd have the last bowlful before I washed the pot, so I dipped it out and set the bowl here on the table while I went out to the smokehouse to fetch a ham. When I returned, she was here by the table, just standing and smiling that queer smile of hers."

"Who? Sybil?"

Bess nodded and clutched her stomach more tightly. " 'Let me fetch you cream for your porridge,' she says and dumps it in the bowl so sweetly. I should have known. 'Tis not like her to wait upon another. Oh, I must lie down."

Rose helped her up to her room and put her to bed. She had heard that death by poisoning was a terrible sight, with the victim retching and thrashing about, but in a few minutes Bess was sound asleep and snoring. Rose felt her brow. It was cool and her face bore the placid look of a sleeping babe. *Whatever might have been in her porridge, it was not a deadly poison,* thought Rose. *Still, if Sybil tried to harm her—.*

She found Sybil dusting in the parlor. "Bess taken ill?" she asked, while her large red hands kept busily wiping objects on the mantle.

"Aye. She insists that there was something in her porridge." Rose waited but Sybil said nothing. "Do you think there could have been something wrong with her porridge?" Rose finally asked.

Sybil turned around and met her gaze. "Nothing but the usual lumps. But why do you ask me? Are you accusing me of trying to harm her?"

"You must agree that you two are not friends."

" 'Tis so, but she is of too little consequence to be considered an enemy. If she—or anyone—were my true enemy, and I wanted to do them harm, then you can be certain I would not let them escape with just a little bellyache." She clenched the featherduster tightly as she spoke, and her whitened knuckles stood out in sharp contrast to her red hands. "Is there something else you wanted?" she asked defiantly. "Do you wish me to prepare the noon meal?"

"I—nay, I fancy cooking it myself today." Rose mumbled and turned and almost ran from the room. *Fie on you,* she told herself, *letting a servant browbeat you. You should have dismissed her long ago. You must replace her and that's that.* She took a deep breath and continued, *But not until Thomas returns.*

Rose was relieved when Bess was fully recovered the next morning. It must have been a simple illness, she thought. But Bess made a grand show of guarding the prepared food in the kitchen whenever Sybil was near.

While Anne was away Rose spent all of her time with Derry. For the first time since he had lost his hearing, she really tried to study his actions and think of ways to communicate with him. But she became impatient one day when she thought he was deliberately ignoring her and she turned him around sharply while she screamed,

"Why won't you obey me?" He had such a sad, confused look on his face that she picked him up and began crying. "I'm sorry, my little one. I want you to learn so much. I just don't know how to teach you."

A tear rolled down her cheek and he caught it with his chubby little finger and wiped it under his own eye. "Nay, nay. We will sorrow no more," she said and kissed the tear away from his face. Then she put him down and said, "Ride horse," exaggerating her lips and holding her hands as if they held reins. He smiled and started for the door.

April and May passed quickly by. Rose missed Thomas and looked forward to his return. *He will be proud of me*, she thought. *I am much calmer now*. She and Derry spent much of their time out-of-doors. She wanted him to see the calving and the cheesemaking, to learn all of the work that went into running the farm. As she visited the women in her knitting guild, she questioned them carefully about any old herbal remedies they might know of and compiled all of their descriptions of plants and herbs that healed. No one had heard of an herb which cured deafness, but she didn't give up her search. As the flowers blossomed and birds sang from every oak tree, she took Derry out to watch them and showed him blue bells and white wood anemone, and the bees swarming around their straw hives.

One morning as they started toward the stable for a ride, Sybil called quietly to her. "Madam, I have good news," she motioned for Rose to follow her to a sheltered corner. When they were out of everyone's hearing she said, "I know a wise woman who has recently come to live near Stanton. She is very skilled in herbs and other remedies. I told her about Master Derry and she says he can easily be healed of his affliction." Sybil kept glancing toward the house as she spoke.

"A wise woman? She's not a witch, is she?"

Sybil licked her thin lips before she replied. "Why madam, you know witchcraft is forbidden and punishable by death. Do you think I would risk punishment by admitting knowledge of one? I only meant to help." She gave Rose a pained look and then her eyes narrowed as she added, "There's no need for Master Stratton to know if you seek her help."

Something in the way she said the last words set off a warning signal in Rose's mind. "I—I'll think on it. She truly said she could heal Derry?"

"Aye, madam."

"As I said, I will consider her offer, but now we must go for our ride and you have work to do." Rose walked toward the stable with Derry skipping alongside her. As she reached the stable she turned around and saw Sybil still standing where she had left her. She had her hands on her hips and was looking straight at Rose, but Rose couldn't make out the expression on Sybil's face. Later she would regret that she hadn't seen it, for it might have warned her of things to come.

Instead of riding her own mount, Rose walked, leading Derry on his little pony to his favorite spot near the spring. It was the middle of June and everything was green. She tied the pony's rein to a bramble bush and showed Derry how to cup his hand and drink the clear, cold water from the spring. She lifted her head when she heard something from the thick woods. *Just some farm worker gathering firewood*, she told herself. After a futile search for tadpoles, she helped Derry climb back up to where the pony was tethered. Something frightened the animal because it whinnied and pulled back, loosening the rein from the bramble bush. "Come back, you silly animal," Rose called as it skitted off. "Derry, help Mama catch the pony," she said and gestured toward the animal. Then she picked up her skirts and ran toward the pony, but again it skitted off. "Pretty pony, here's something to eat." She held out her hand as if to give him a treat but he bolted away just as she tried to grab the loose reins. She followed, laughing. "Naughty pony, I don't want to carry your little master all the way home. Here, Derry, you—"

She turned around and found that Derry was not right behind her as she had thought, but was running toward the woods. She had started walking toward him when she saw a movement in the thick stand of birches just ahead of Derry. A pack of wild dogs was emerging from the woods. There were five of them—two black and three a dirty yellow. The large, hungry-looking mongrels had just spotted Derry and were glaring menacingly as they moved toward him.

"Derry, stop! Come here!" she cried as she ran toward her son, knowing all the while he couldn't hear her. The leader of the pack slowly approached Derry, teeth bared, his head low to the ground. Rose was still a good distance away from Derry, but she waved her arms as she ran, trying to frighten the dogs away. "Please, dear Lord!" she begged in desperation. "Let me reach him in time. Please save him!" She stumbled and fell flat on her face. She was dazed for a moment and then clutched at the grass, pulling herself up just in time to see the lead dog almost reach Derry.

Suddenly a stone hurled past her and struck the dog sharply in the head. He yelped and stopped in his tracks.

"Get away, you scruffy hounds!" called a voice behind her as another stone found its mark. The leader turned away and with his tail tucked between his legs, ran back into the woods, with the rest of the pack following.

Rose ran quickly to Derry and when he was safely in her arms, turned around to thank their rescuer. "Tad! You saved Derry's life!"

The stableboy turned red. " 'Twas nothing. I seen the pony heading back t' the stable and knowed something was amiss. I knew this is Master Derry's favorite spot so—" he shrugged off the rest of his rescue, but Rose knew he would tell and retell it in great detail to the other servants.

"You're a clever lad and I'm sure Master Thomas will reward you handsomely when he hears of your quick actions."

Tad blushed with pride. "Once I saw a hungry pack tear a young lamb t' bits."

Rose shuddered and felt faint. "Here," she told Tad, "You'd best carry the child." She looked over her shoulder, but there was no sign of the wild dogs. "We'll hurry home and I'll have Humfrey take some men and rid our woods of those beasts."

That night she lay awake thinking of Derry's close call. Her earlier prayer of submission to God was all but forgotten. Once again she began taking matters into her own hands. Surely, she could find the answer for Derry. *How many times,* she wondered, *will someone call out to warn Derry of danger and he will not hear? I've grown complacent. I must find a cure for him. Whatever it takes, I must.*

The next day she waited for a time when she could converse with Sybil in private. At last the moment came when Sybil was changing linens. She had remade Rose and Thomas's great featherbed and was smoothing out the coverlet with a stick.

"Sybil," Rose said softly.

"Yea, madam?"

Rose closed the door quietly and came close to Sybil. "This wise woman you spoke of—" Sybil stopped her work and turned slowly around to face Rose. She arched her eyebrows and smiled as she waited for Rose to finish. "This wise woman—do you think you could go and fetch her for me?"

"Nay, madam. She would never leave her dwelling and come here. She shuns strangers and only sees people that her friends send to her."

"I would think that a woman so wise would be eager to help others."

"Oh, she is, she is, but several prominent physicians were jealous of her skills and sought to do her harm, so she retreated to safety. If I tell you were she lives, you must promise not to reveal it to anyone."

A warning voice inside Rose told her to turn and walk out, but as she hesitated Sybil spoke again.

"I heard that little Master Derry was almost killed yesterday."

Rose took a deep breath. "The wise woman. I will go to her. Now tell me where she lives."

Sybil was silent for a moment, but Rose could tell by the way her eyes darted back and forth that she was devising a plan. At last the maidservant said, "I know that Master Derry is your great treasure—worth far more to you than all your jewels. She held out her empty hands. "I have no such treasure"—her hand went to the neckline of her dress—"not even one ruby broach."

Without a word, Rose turned to seek out Humfrey to fetch the jewel. In the past months she had never given it a thought but it was apparent Sybil had. *The evil, conniving wench,* Rose thought as she walked, *but she speaks the truth on one matter: Derry is my treasure, my only treasure, and his happiness is everything to me. Nothing else matters. Nothing.*

Chapter Fifteen

"WHAT KIND OF a mother would I be if I failed to try every means to heal Derry. This wise woman may know of some rare herbs that heal. Didn't Sybil say she was from the north somewhere?" As she rode toward the village of Stanton, Rose continued justifying her mission. She hadn't asked God's guidance. If she were honest with herself, she would admit she didn't want to know His will in this matter.

Rose followed Sybil's instructions and took Bury Lane to Stanton and then rode through a deep hollow pathway known as Stanton Grundle. There were steep banks on both sides of the gravelly path with tall birches making a canopy of leaves. The shadowy trail added to her sense of foreboding. *I'm not saying I will accept her remedy. I am merely exploring another possibility. Sybil is a superstitious, foolish woman, but that doesn't mean this wise woman is like her.*

Once out of the grundle she relaxed and enjoyed the fine June morning. She rode past several scattered cottages and came to a small track that led into a grove. Rose dismounted and pretended to rest Brownie while she looked up and down the lane. Assured that no one was approaching from either direction, she led her horse down the track.

After about ten minutes she came to what once must have been a woodsman's cottage. Woodbine had crept across the sides of the cottage, half concealing it, and the thatched roof was covered with a thick layer of dead leaves. It was as if the cottage had reverted back to nature and was itself a living plant. Rose raised her hand to knock on the door just as it was opened.

"You're Mistress Stratton. Come in. I've been expecting you."

Rose had envisioned the wise woman as a hump-backed old crone with a wart on her chin. She was taken aback by the genteel appearance of the woman who greeted her. She was tall and slender, and although her unbound hair was completely gray, she had an unlined face with regular features. Her skin was pale, almost transparent. Her brows and lashes were also pale, almost white in fact, and she steadily regarded Rose with very light blue eyes.

When Rose stepped inside, the woman shut and bolted the door. Even in the dim light of a small hearth fire, Rose could see that the cottage was tidy and normal looking, except for a rather large amount of bunches of herbs drying. She had braced herself for strange disgusting odors like in an apothecary's shop, but there was just a pleasant scent from a pan of pottage bubbling on the hearth. The wise woman motioned for Rose to sit down on an ordinary bench by an ordinary trestle table. Rose began to feel foolish for dreading this meeting. She jumped as something furry rubbed against her leg.

"Bran, begone!" The woman shooed a black cat out from under the table. She gave Rose a smile, "There's no need to fear. Now tell me about your son. Derry, isn't it? You should have brought him with you, you know." She knelt down and stirred the pottage in slow rhythmic motions.

The action soothed Rose somehow and she began, "I had journeyed to Norwich, leaving my son in another's care and he fell ill and—I don't even know your name—"

"You may call me Joanna. But please continue." Joanna sat on the floor with the agility of a cat, resting her chin on her knees. Almost in spite of herself Rose told her the whole story, even about her pilgrimage to Newgate Prison. After she finished Joanna made no reply, so Rose said impatiently, "Well, Sybil said you knew a remedy. Do you or not?"

Joanna waited another moment and then replied, "You are rich. You must have sought out all the great physicians."

"Aye, to no avail."

"And you fasted and prayed, and yet in spite of all you've suffered, God has not answered you," Joanna said softly. "You think He no longer cares about you or your son."

"What?" Rose blushed. It was as if the woman had read her thoughts, and hearing them expressed aloud made Rose feel so ashamed. "I—I must go." She started for the door.

Joanna made no move to stop her but sighed, adding, "How sad for a child to be consigned to a silent world. He'll be treated as if he were mad, you know. A thing without a brain, an outcast." Her voice turned bitter as she continued, "Aye, he might even be forced to live apart as I do to be rid of the mockers with their gibes and stones."

At the mention of stones, the memory of Derry being pelted with pebbles by Mirabel's children flashed in Rose's mind. She hesitated at the door. "Mayhap," said Joanna, "your God has answered your prayer by sending you to me for help."

Rose cried out in desperation, "Oh, can you help him? Can you?" When Joanna failed to reply, Rose continued in a whisper, "Is there no hope at all?"

Joanna stood up and slowly came to face Rose. She took her hand and said, "There is hope. You have come to the only person who can give you hope. I know the old ways of healing, the ways of the ancient ones."

The soft sound of her voice began to frighten Rose and she said, "Tell me not how you came by your cures. I will pay you handsomely if you—"

"Pay? I do not take payment. Do not even speak of it. My powers are a gift. Now you must bring your child to me and leave him here for seven days."

"Nay, I could not." Rose recoiled at the thought. "If you must see him, then come with me to my home."

They stood staring into each other's eyes. Rose almost gave way and agreed to bring Derry, and then she set her chin and stood her ground.

"Very well," said Joanna. "I will give you a potion, but I cannot be as certain of its effect if I cannot watch him constantly."

"Tell me what to do."

The woman had brought out two packets from her pocket as though she had prepared them for Rose. "It is not only what you must do, but what you must say that is important."

"But why must I say words?" Rose backed toward the door again.

"Sounds are a part of life; the particular sound of the nightingale—the sounds of the beasts differ one from another. All the sounds of nature are different and important, the sounds that your dear son may never hear. Sound is an important part in healing. Why, even the sound of a baby's cry brings milk to its mother's breast. Is not the Christ called the Word?"

"Aye, but—"

Joanna held back the packets. "Do not take the remedy unless you swear to say the words."

"Tell me them first."

Joanna said them. *A string of jibberish*, Rose thought. *No harm to that. There was no mention of Satan or demons or other evil in them. Mayhap it was just an old language that had been passed down from generation to generation.*

"Very well, I so swear," said Rose. Once outside, she quickly mounted her horse and urged him over the narrow track and out onto the open lane. As she rode she kept looking back over her shoulder as if the ominous presence she had felt in the cottage was following her. When she neared the manor, she slowed her horse to a walk while she calmed herself.

At suppertime Sybil cast her several knowing looks, but Rose didn't volunteer any information concerning her trip to Joanna's cottage. She had decided that although Joanna wouldn't accept payment for cures, she would reward Sybil if Derry were healed, but for now she kept quiet about it.

Rose took Derry to her own bedchamber and sat with him by the fireplace until he fell asleep. She watched out the windeye until the moon seemed to be at its height. Joanna had said the remedy must be applied then. A soft, fragrant breeze was blowing, and she heard an owl call in the distance. After placing the sleeping child in her bed, Rose removed the two packets from her jewelry chest where she had hidden them and emptied them into a small saucelier, adding a few drops of water as Joanna had instructed. Then she warmed the mixture over the embers until it became a dark red paste. With a trembling hand she dipped her handkerchief into the mixture and painted the paste on Derry's left ear and then his right.

He stirred slightly and tried to pull her hand away, but she petted him until he was fast asleep again. Then came the part she dreaded. *I have gone this far*, she thought, *I must finish the remedy*. She turned Derry on his back and cupped her hands lightly over his ears as she said the words Joanna had made her memorize. "La eh won peed fo dog," she whispered and then said it once more in louder tones. "La eh won peed fo dog." She held her hands over his ears for a moment longer until he rolled to his side. Joanna had instructed her not to awaken him to see if he was cured, for the potion might take hours to work itself into the ears. She wiped the rest of the paste out of the saucelier with her handkerchief and threw it into the embers. This caused a billow of black smoke to swirl up into the chimney. Trembling again, Rose closed the windeye and lay down beside Derry and fell alseep.

Well past dawn she awoke and saw that Derry was not in bed. She sat up and was relieved to see him sitting in the corner playing with her jewelry chest. She jumped out of bed and called, "Derry, come here." He turned around immediately and ran to her. She scooped him up in her arms. "Oh, you can hear. You can hear!" She began crying and rocked him back and forth in her arms. "Oh, my dear child. Now I can teach you so much, and you need never endure— Who is it?" Rose set Derry on the bed and opened the door. Anne rushed in and curtsied. "My pardon, madam, but I thought Derry would like to see—twin calves have been born and Master Humfrey has them in the courtyard."

"I've more wonderous news than that," Rose told her. "Derry can hear! He's been healed. Haven't you, my dearling?"

Derry was playing with a coral necklace and didn't look up. "Derry, look at me!" Rose shouted. Still he gave no notice.

"His ears. Is that blood on his ears?" asked Anne in alarm.

"Nay, just leave us."

"I might not have mixed the powders properly," Rose mumbled after Anne left the room. "Oh, how foolish of me to throw the rest away. Mayhap the moon was not at its height. I could take Derry to Joanna's cottage. The words. I might not have said them properly." She stepped to the desk and took out a piece of foolscap, dipped the quill into the inkhorn and tried to write out the words as Joanna had spoken them. "La eh won peed fo dog." Dog. That was the only recognizable word in the phrase. She wondered why it was in the midst of all the unintelligible sounds. *Mayhap the powders contained the ground bone of a dog*, she thought. *After all, dogs are known for their keen hearing. Aye, that must be it.* She felt uneasy and stared at the words again. "D-o-g" backward became "god." A chill ran through her as she reversed the next group of letters. "f-o" became "of." She dipped her quill again into the inkhorn and wrote out the entire phrase in reverse order. It became "god of deep now he al." She said it aloud. "God of deep now he al—heal. God of deep now heal." She dropped the quill and tipped over her stool as she stood up. "Oh, Lord, oh, Lord!" she cried, "Forgive me. Oh, Father, I have been so blind, so spiritually blind. How could I have sought out that evil woman's help? It was as if I were seeking after other gods. And she did beguile me into praying to her false gods. Lord, cleanse my mouth from speaking those horrible words." She grabbed Derry and scrubbed the last traces of the red paste from his ears. He cried and fought her, but she calmed him down and sat on the bed with him while she searched through the Bible. "Oh, Father," she prayed as she leafed through the pages. "I can clean the potion from his flesh, but only you can guard him and keep him from evil. Lord, cover us with your blood that was shed on Calvary." Her eyes fell on Isaiah 8:19: "And when they shall say unto you, Seek unto them that have familiar spirits, and unto wizards that peep, and that mutter: should not a people seek unto their God?" Then she turned to Deuteronomy 18 and read verses 10 through 13: "There shall not be found among you any one that maketh his son or his daughter to pass through the fire, or that useth divination or an observer of times, or an enchanter, or a witch, or a charmer, or a consulter with familiar spirits, or a wizard, or a necromancer. For all that do these things are an abomination unto the Lord: and because of these abominations the Lord thy God doth drive them out from before thee. Thou shalt be perfect with the Lord thy God."

"Lord, my greatest sin was my anger toward you." She continued on for some time reading scriptures aloud and praying until she felt free from the resentment, frustration and anger of the past month.

She knew God had forgiven her and now she was filled with a different kind of anger, a righteous anger. She calmly carried Derry into the nursery and handed him to Anne. Then she marched downstairs in search of Sybil. She found her scrubbing the porch steps.

"You knew, didn't you?" Rose asked her.

Sybil looked up with a sly smile on her face. "Knew what, madam?"

"That Joanna was a witch. She had me say an incantation to false gods."

Sybil laughed and stood up, casually dropping her scrub brush into the bucket of soapy water so that it splashed on Rose's gown.

"Tell me you knew," Rose insisted.

"Aye, I knew she was a witch and so did you. Holy, holy, holy aren't we—until our prayers go unanswered. You're not fit to be Derry's mother. He should belong to me." Sybil had screwed up her face into the very picture of hatred. The force of her accusation stunned Rose until she remembered that "we wrestle not with flesh and blood, but against principalities, against powers, against the rulers of the darkness of this world, against spiritual wickedness in high places." Rose said quietly, "My sins have been forgiven and washed away in the blood of Jesus, and no one, *no one*, has any right to accuse me of them."

Sybil's face turned back to its usual impassive mask. "Now," said Rose, breathing easier, "I order you to leave my house by dawn tomorrow. I shall leave a month's wages for you with Humfrey, but by the time I arise, I want you to be off our land. Until morning, keep out of my sight!"

Sybil hurried off toward the stable.

Chapter Sixteen

LATER, WHEN Sybil had shut herself up in her bedchamber, Rose went to the stable to get Brownie.

She had to get away from the house, to avoid the stares of the servants. By now, as she rode her horse down the lane through the village and toward Bury, Sybil had certainly told the entire household of her visit to the witch. What would Anne think of her? She was responsible to teach the girl godly ways. What an example she had set by seeking after evil cures.

As she allowed accusing thoughts to enter her mind, others soon followed, swooping into her mind like bats. She even fancied as she rode on more deserted paths that she could smell their sickly sweet scents. As she rode south, she reached open land, where even in the midsummer there was little vegetation, just blowing sand and the glint of flints reflecting the sun. Horrible scenes flashed before her mind as she rode: a traitor being drawn and quartered, John Newman's hair ablaze as his head fell into the flames at the stake, her beloved Derick being beaten to the ground by his captors, the wicked face of the jailer's wife when she vowed to keep Rose's baby. Sounds from the past assailed her also. Crackling flames, screams, cries of despair, *cries*—she realized that she was crying aloud. She reined her horse up and looked around. Which way led home? As she slackened on the reins, Brownie began slowly heading down one path. She saw a landmark and realized she was on the right path. "Good, Brownie." She patted her horse's neck, and slackening the reins, let him lead her home.

"Rub him down and give him an extra measure of oats," she told Tad when she dismounted at the stable door. "He's an intelligent beast." As she walked to the house, she was calm again. Tomorrow morning Sybil would be gone and things would get back to normal. *I'll begin Bible studies with the servants again, and if I must, I'll confess my sin to them and*—"Oh, Thomas!"

He was riding up the drive. Seeing him she ran into the garden, blushing with shame. How could she ever face him?

"Rose!" he called after her. "What is it?" She ran to the corner of the garden and was sobbing when he approached.

"My dear, what—" He tried to take her in his arms.

"Don't touch me, Thomas. Unclean. Unclean—" she backed away from him, stumbled and fell to the ground. He knelt down beside her. "Are you ill?" he asked as he tried to lift her.

She pushed his hands away and sat up with her back to him. Her voice broke as she said, "I've sinned most grievously, Thomas, and I will not blame you if you never wish to see me again."

"But what—"

"Thomas, I sought the help of a witch to cure Derry." Her voice rushed on, "Oh, I didn't know at the time, at least I didn't admit it to myself, but I was so desperate, so hopeless and—" He listened in silence as she told him of the wild dogs, going to the witch's cottage and the backward spell. "And there it is. I am an unfit mother for Derry, I know. You must loathe to look upon me."

"Oh, my dearling," he said and helped her to stand and then held her tightly for a moment. "When you began, for a moment I thought— you are so beautiful and I was gone so long—I thought you were telling me you had found another love."

"Oh, never, never! I love you. And Thomas, I deceived you when we were last in London. Remember when Derry and I returned the morning of my brother's arrival, and I said we had only been out for a walk? We had actually been to Newgate Prison." From there Rose explained her false hope in a pilgrimage and how she had lied to get free from the keeper. Then she remembered Sybil and knew the danger was very real that the servant might dredge up the lie about her and Edmund Laxton, so she told Thomas all about it.

"Concerning the lie, I certainly forgive you. And about Sybil, if only you had told me then. I would have dismissed her on the spot. How could I take her word against yours? As for this witch, aye, 'twas wrong for you to seek her, but I blame myself also. I do leave you alone too much. And the trip to Spain, it was not all that necessary. I just did not know how to help you. It seemed my presence angered you, somehow. Oh, but dearling, I have good news for you. My trip to Spain was not entirely in vain. I have heard of a monk in Vallidolid, who has done miracles with deaf children."

"He can restore their hearing?" she asked excitedly.

"Nay, nay, that you must put aside once and for all. He cannot restore their hearing, but he can teach them to read and write and speak. The city is in the interior of Spain. English merchants are granted the rights to dwell only in Cadiz and Seville, but I have employed an interpreter to journey to see this monk, Pedro do Ponce, and try to obtain a written description of his methods."

"But what if he will not divulge his teaching methods?" she asked.

"Nevertheless, it shows that there is a way to train Derry and we shall find it, together. I was wrong not to encourage you to train him; I see that now. Will you forgive me?"

"Of course! But what of my sin? I've sought after false gods."

"Have you asked the Lord to forgive you, Rose?"

"Of course, but—"

"Then the only one who would accuse you is Satan, and he has no right. Your sins have been washed away and God remembers them no more. 'As far as the east is from the west, so far hath He removed our transgressions from us.' Do you believe that scripture?

"Aye, but—"

"Then when accusations come, they have no right to stay. Tell your accuser that the sin has been washed away and he will flee."

"Thomas, I've still so much to learn about the Christian walk."

"I too, my dear, but we must always walk together."

"Papa." Little Derry toddled up to them and hugged Thomas's leg. "Papa," he said again. Anne was close behind him.

"But, Anne, how—" begged Rose.

"He remembered the word. I just helped him form his lips to say it as a surprise for the master. He is very bright, madam."

"Aye, indeed he is, and you are a clever girl to help him. We're going to teach him many things."

At supper they were served by Bess who murmured all the while about Sybil staying in her room and not helping her. "We shall hire another maidservant, Bess," Thomas comforted her, "a Christian woman."

"Just so's she knows how to clean—" replied Bess.

Late in the night as Rose stared up into the blackness, the accusing thought assailed her again. This time the faces of Sybil and Joanna seemed to swoop down at her, their expressions taunting and evil. She felt as if she were paralyzed, helpless against the onslaught, and then with great effort she moved her lips and whispered, "Jesus is Lord." She felt free and then said loudly, "My sins have been forgiven and washed away by the blood of the Lamb, Jesus, Son of the Most High God, and you have no right to accuse me." She relaxed and breathed deeply as Thomas stirred. Then she lit a taper in the embers of the fireplace and fetched her Bible. In the dim light she turned to Isaiah and read, "Thou wilt keep him in perfect peace, whose mind is stayed on thee: because he trusteth in thee." As she continued reading the Scriptures aloud, it was as if all the accusing and oppressing spirits had retreated at the sound of the truth. She read for a while longer and then wanted to wake Thomas and tell him of the victory, but he was sleeping soundly. "Sleep well, my darling," she said softly. It was the first time she had called him that, and she meant it with all her heart. She extinguished the candle and crawled back into bed, falling asleep quickly.

She awoke in the morning to the sound of Anne's urgent call. "Madam, Sir, may I enter?"

"Of course," Rose replied. "What's amiss? Is Derry ill?"

The girl peeked inside and then staggered through the door. She was still in her nightclothes. "I hoped he was with you, but the Master being home and—oh, my head."

Rose jumped from the bed and ran to the swaying girl. "What is it? You can't find Derry?"

Anne shook her head, a look of anguish on her face.

"Thomas, awaken!" Rose shouted and then rushed into the nursery. Derry was nowhere in sight and his favorite coverlet was missing.

Anne had followed her and slumped down on her own cot. "The last thing I remember was Sybil coming in at bedtime to bid me farewell. She brought me a mug of cider and—"

"Sybil!" Rose climbed the stairs to the garret and threw open the door to Sybil's room. The flock mattress was rolled up in the corner and all her belongings were gone.

Thomas was pulling on his boots when Rose ran back into the bedchamber. "What is amiss?" he inquired. "Has Derry strayed away?"

"Not strayed, stolen!" cried Rose. " 'Tis Sybil's doing, I know it. She is getting back at me for dismissing her. Oh, 'tis all my fault." She began pacing the floor and wringing her hands. "Hurry! We must ride after them."

"Calm yourself," Thomas told her as he followed her downstairs. "We must search the grounds thoroughly first. Sybil might merely have left at dawn as you ordered her to do, and Derry might be down at the stables or one of the other outbuildings. You and Anne look in the garden while I gather the men to search the grounds."

Rose and Anne looked behind every hedge and bush in the large garden and were entering the courtyard when Thomas met them. "Brownie and his saddle are missing, too," he said shortly. "I fear Sybil must have him. I'll leave some men to search the grounds, and Humfrey and I and five others are saddling up to find her trail." He looked up at the thickening clouds. "I hope we can find it before the rain breaks. You stay inside and wait for the word."

Rose grabbed his arm, "Wait? I cannot rest here while my son may be in mortal danger. Saddle me another horse. I'm going with you."

She quickly dressed and was coming downstairs when the storm broke with a huge roll of thunder. She pulled the hood of her cape over her head and went out into the downpour. "There will be no hope of following a trail now," Thomas told her as he helped her mount up. "We shall have to divide the searchers, half on the road to Bury and half toward Stowmarket."

"Nay, send one or two on those paths, but you and the rest follow me," she said over the driving downpour. "I believe I know where she is taking him."

After thoroughly soaking both riders and horses, the rain stopped and sunlight began spreading glitter on the wet foliage and the puddles in Bury Lane. When they reached the village of Stanton, Thomas had his men knock on doors and ask if anyone had seen a woman and child riding through, but no one had any information.

The air had become quite cold for late June and puffs of moisture were coming from the horses' nostrils as their riders forced them on. As Rose led them down the trail to Joanna's cottage, she felt a terrible dread come upon her. She was the first to dismount, but Thomas caught her arm and ordered her to stand well back as he kicked open the cottage door. There was no sign of life in the cottage. Even the hearthstone was cold. "Oh, those wicked women! Where have they taken my son?" Rose cried.

Thomas comforted her and then called to Humfrey. "Ride back to Stanton," he told the overseer, "and ask the villagers if there is some henge monument or other ancient place nearby where the old religion was practiced. And this time offer a reward to anyone who might have information that will help us find my son."

"The rest of you men fan out in the woods," he ordered, "and search for their tracks."

Rose scoured the cottage for clues that would show if Sybil had indeed brought Derry there but she found nothing. There was an oaken chest shoved back in the corner and the lid had closed on a bit of faded scarlet fabric. She opened the chest and pulled out a scarlet cape. Underneath it lay a jumble of old garments, but she saw a bit of leather and pulled out a belt which held a sheath containing a knife. Rose gingerly loosed the knife from its sheath and examined it. On the ivory handle was carved the face of a malevolent-looking goat. The blade was serpentine-shaped with both curving edges razor sharp. She carried the belt to the lighted doorway to get a better look and gasped. She called Thomas and showed him the indentation where another twin sheath had fit. Together they pulled out all the contents of the chest but didn't find the other knife. "Thomas, last night was the summer solstice—Could it be?"

His face was grim as he replied, "Don't even think it! No one would sacrifice an innocent child."

Chapter Seventeen

"SIR." HUMFREY HAD returned. "One of the graybeards in the village told of a spring not far from here that in olden times was sacred to Epona the horse goddess. Might not the witch have resorted to such a place?"

"A place of sacrifice!" cried Rose. "Hasten, oh, hasten!"

The searchers quickly mounted and followed Humfrey as he led them back down the path toward Stanton, then turned into a small track that led through a meadow. The track led them through another thick wood and into a clearing. In the center of the clearing stood a hillock that Rose thought must have been manmade centuries past, but was now so overgrown with grass and brush that it blended into the natural landscape. A blackbird, happy that the rain had stopped, was whistling in an oak tree at the edge of the clearing. The scene was so lovely that for a moment Rose felt encouraged. Surely no evil had taken place in such a beautiful spot, she told herself.

"I've found the spring," called one of the farmhands from the far side of the hillock. Rose and Thomas joined the others as they came upon a ring of stones which surrounded a small bubbling spring. A path around the stones had been trampled in the grass by many footprints. A small pile of soggy ashes lay a few yards away.

"They were here, those wicked women! Where can they have taken him?"

"Over here!" another servant called from the edge of the clearing. "More footprints and the tracks from many horses."

"Many horses?" asked Rose. "Joanna had no horses. There should

142

be just the tracks from Brownie, and yet, we found no fresh tracks at Joanna's cottage."

"Master Stratton," Humfrey called in a low but commanding voice. He was standing on top of the hillock and staring down at something. The expression on his face chilled Rose's heart.

Thomas gripped her shoulder and said tersely, "Wait here," and he bounded up the hillock. Rose, after a moment's hesitation, followed behind him. When she reached the top, the two men had their backs to her and were standing motionless, looking down at the large flat rock in front of them. Rose pushed between them, dreading what she might see and yet compelled to look.

At first she sighed with relief. All she saw was the wet, gray stone and little pools of rainwater which had been trapped in several hollow spots. And then she looked closer. In a narrow fissure that ran diagonally across one corner of the stone lay a flesh colored object covered by pink water. She screamed as she identifed the object. It was a length of entrails.

Thomas held her tightly, but she struggled wildly within his grasp. "Release me, release me!" she cried. She pulled free and flung herself down beside the stone. "Oh, God! oh, God! The monsters, they've killed my baby! I don't want to live. I don't want to draw another breath! She struck the stone over and over with her fist until Thomas had to grab her bloodied hand and with Humfrey's help, lead her away from the terrible sight. The other searchers looked away helplessly as the three reached the foot of the hillock.

"Halloo." A man's voice rang from the woods. "Are you looking for the witches?" A woodsman appeared at the edge of the clearing and leaned on his axe as he continued, "Squire Mortimer has already captured them and taken them in to Bury. Fair bursting with anger he was that they had slaughtered one of his ewes for their heathen rites."

"A ewe?" Thomas asked with an unsteady voice. "It was a sheep they sacrificed? Are you certain of this?"

"Aye," replied the man, stepping closer. "I was gathering wood in yon thicket at dawn when I spied the three of them asleep right on this hillock. I sneaked up to have a closer look and I saw the poor dead beast all carved up on that rock. I hastened to tell the squire, 'tis his land, and he brought his men and apprehended the three witches before they could flee. He gave me a coin for my troubles, he did.''

Rose had heard the man speak without comprehending what he said, so deep was her black pool of sorrow. Thomas shook her gently. "Dearling, did you hearken to the man? 'Twas a sheep that was slain, not—'' Thomas shuddered and his voice broke as he said, "Praise God it was not him.'' They held each other for a moment and then Rose wiped her hand across her brow as if erasing that horrible vision. She took hold of the woodsman's sleeve. "A child. Was there a child with them? A little boy? Oh, tell me,'' she demanded.

The woodsman looked bewildered. "N—nay, madam. There was just the three.''

"Describe them for me, please.''

He continued slowly, "There was the one, the chief witch, I reckon. She was tall and had gray hair and wore a black robe. The other woman was old and hump-backed, an ugly bag of bones. And there was a young man, he seemed to be a half-wit.''

"No other? Not a woman with red hair?''

"Nay, madam, just the three.''

She whirled about. "Thomas, if Sybil didn't take Derry to Joanna, then where are they? Oh, we've lost precious time.'' She walked over to her horse and stood beside him, swaying as she tried to mount.

"Dearling, listen to me,'' Thomas said as he took the reins from her hands. "I am sending you home with Humfrey. There's nothing more we can do in this area. I'll ride into Bury and question this Joanna. Mayhap Sybil did come to her before she carried Derry off to another hiding place. You must go home and wait for me.''

"I cannot,'' she replied in a weak voice. "I must search.''

"Rose, listen. What if one of the other searchers finds Derry and brings him to the manor and you are not there? I pray you, do as I say. I'll bring news as soon as I can.''

She put her hand to her forehead and nodded as she answered in a quavering voice. "Home. Aye, I must go home. Derry might be there even now.''

It was early afternoon when she and Humfrey rode into the courtyard. Anne rushed out to greet them, but her look of anticipation turned to sorrow as she saw that Derry was not with them. She followed Rose upstairs and helped her change into dry clothing. Rose was grateful that she didn't ask any questions, although later when she looked out of the nursery window, she saw Anne and the cook talking to Humfrey.

Rose waited in the nursery for Thomas's return. She was so weary she could not even pray coherently, but just thought, *Oh, Lord, oh, Lord, oh, Lord,* over and over in her mind. She sat on the edge of Derry's bed and clutched his little pillow to her breast.

It was dark when she heard the sound of hoofbeats. Thomas and the others had returned, and Rose rushed down to meet him. He looked exhausted too and there were deep lines in his face as he shook his head in reply to her questioning look. "No news at all. The coven was questioned for hours and under threat of torture, but I'm convinced that they know nothing of Sybil's whereabouts. The man is obviously half-witted and bewitched by the fleshly charms of this Joanna more than by any evil spells. The old crone is an embittered, evil-hearted creature who would love to put a curse on all humanity. Only Joanna could be called a true worshiper of Satan. She boasted that she—well it matters not."

"Nay, tell me."

"She boasted that she had enticed a Christian into witchcraft. She even spoke your name, but no one took notice. She had venomous accusations for everyone present."

"She did not entice me. I deceived myself. Do you suppose God has taken Derry away to punish me?"

"Rose, we are both weary. Pray do not continue this self-incrimination. We must rest and make a fresh start tomorrow. I've enlisted more men to join the search in the morning. Come up to bed now."

"I cannot. How can I lay my head on a soft pillow while Derry may be shivering in the forest or tied up on the straw in some hut? Or worse, what if Sybil has abandoned him and he is wandering in the darkness? Oh, Father in Heaven, I cannot bear it." She turned from him and started for the door. "I must find him, I must."

Thomas had to forcibly restrain her, holding her tightly as she wept. "Let me carry you to bed, dearling." Again she refused to go upstairs and so he left her sitting in the parlor, staring into the fire.

Rose awoke with a start. Sunlight was streaming through the windeye. She rubbed her stiff neck and realized that she had slept the night away in her chair. "Thomas, Thomas," she called.

Bess appeared. Her face was lined with concern. "Master Stratton has taken Humfrey and some other men to continue the search, madam. He said we was to let you sleep as long as possible. I didn't wake you by my clattering the pans, did I?"

"Nay, but I must overtake them. I cannot abide here." She opened the door and heard a horse whinny. *It must be Thomas returning*, she thought. But then she gasped, "Brownie." The riderless horse trotted right up to the porch steps. His reins hung loose. He was frothy with sweat and his flanks bore fresh scratches as if he had run through bramble bushes. "There, there, boy," she soothed as she caught hold of the reins. "You're home now." She led him to the stables and began wiping him down. "Oh, if you could only speak. You could tell me where Derry is. What does this mean? Your coming back alone. Did you throw them? Is Derry lying injured on some lonely path? They mustn't be too far away or you would never have found your way back. Oh, Brownie, help me find them."

"I'll help you, madam."

"What? Oh, Tad, I didn't see you."

"I have my own hidey hole in yonder stall," he said with a sly grin. "When I wearies of 'Tad do this' and 'Tad do that,' I hide so's no one can find me." He patted Brownie on the muzzle. "I asked to go search with Master this morning, but he said to stay and help you. So how shall I help you, madam?"

"I know not—stay, mayhap you can. Two days ago when I bade Sybil to leave, she stalked off toward the stable. Did you see her?"

"Nay, but I heard her well enough."

"You were in your hidey hole?"

"Aye, but don't tell Master Humfrey. He'll cane me if he finds I hide from him."

"No one will punish you. Just tell me what you heard."

He turned red. "Just a string of oaths I daren't repeat to a lady. She cursed you roundly and said—" he looked uncomfortable.

"Tad, have mercy, tell me."

"She said she'd take Master Derry straight to hell. I didn't know she would carry 'im off like she did or I would have warned you, madam. I didn't know—"

Rose patted the boy's shoulder. "Fret not. You're not to blame. The blame is mine. Think carefully. Is that all she said? There was no clue as to where she would go? Straight to hell—what can that mean except she plans to kill him. Oh, Lord, oh, Lord, protect him. Why do I stand here talking? I must search, but where? where?"

Tad's face was screwed up into a caricature of concentration.

"Here, here, I think I've found it. Sybil didn't say she would take him straight to hell; she said she would take him to the mouth of hell."

"So? The meaning is the same."

" 'Tis not. Mistress, the mouth of hell. I know exactly where it is."

It was all Rose could do to keep from urging Brownie into a gallop as she followed the path Tad had indicated, but she knew she had to pace the weary animal or he might give out before she reached her destination. She had refused to wait for Tad to saddle another horse. Besides, she didn't want to trust a strange mount when riding alone over unknown terrain. Poor Tad. He had wanted to lead her to the cave himself, but she had ordered him to wait for Thomas's return.

A light, misty rain began falling, and she wrapped her cloak about her and felt for the leather pouch which hung from the saddle. It contained several torches and the flint with which to light them. From Tad's description, the cave led deep into the earth. She shivered as she thought of Derry, frightened and crying in such a place. Unconsciously she had dug her heels into Brownie's sides and was urging him into a fast canter.

Several miles to the north of the manor, the path led through grundle, this one more deep and overgrown than the one Rose had followed to Joanna's cottage. She was not afraid, this time, of riding through the shadowy, ditch-like grundle. At last she had a definite clue to Derry's whereabouts, and it gave her a surge of energy to know she was nearing the cave. She felt as if nothing could frighten or slow her from her mission. When knots of fear about her son's welfare started to rise within her, she determinedly forced them down.

She refused to be paralyzed by dread. *Whatever it takes to free him from Sybil's clutches, that, by the grace of God, I will do*, she thought.

The grundle was over half a mile long and as the ditch widened out near its exit, she found the mouth of hell. It looked insignificant at first glance. It seemed as if some giant had playfully gouged out a smiling mouth from the steep bank of the grundle. Grass and bushes grew about the upper lip of the opening, giving the cave's entrance a humorous, grandfatherly appearance.

Brownie shied and whinnied as they approached the entrance, and she gave him a reassuring pat and then dismounted. She could see footprints in the soft earth leading to the entrance which was about five feet up from the grundle's floor. She bit her lip to keep from calling out to Sybil. If Sybil did indeed have Derry in the cave, then surprise would be her best weapon. She tied Brownie's reins to a young oak.

Her heart was pounding as she crouched under the shelter of the oak and lit one of her torches. The rain had begun to fall heavily and she shielded her torch with her cape as she climbed up into the mouth of the cave. The entrance was about ten feet wide and only four feet in height, so she ducked her head and stepped quickly inside. The cave entrance opened up into a chamber much wider and a few feet higher and she was able to stand upright. She held the torch out before her and could see that the chamber was empty. The ceiling sloped down toward the far back and seemed to extend some yards beyond the light of the torch. She walked carefully toward the back and bent her head to avoid a low ledge of stone and then caught herself just in time as the floor of the cave dropped off into nothingness. *The mouth of hell was aptly named*, she thought. The floor of the cave had veered slightly upward seeming to meet the back wall and so by a trick of nature, an unsuspecting man or animal could walk off into an abyss.

With trembling legs she knelt down and held her torch out over the black pit. Below was a larger chamber stretching out underneath the one she was in. About twenty feet down she could see a natural bridge about three feet wide lying across another chasm. *Oh, Father in Heaven, did they both fall into that pit? Nay, what is that?* She crept over to the right side of the cave and the torchlight revealed a ledge that descended down to the bridge. It was very narrow, but it could be managed. An odd, unpleasant odor wafted up to her, the odor of sulfur and bats. *This is truly the mouth of hell. I might not come back alive if I go down there,* she thought. *But if my son is down there—*She hitched her skirts up in her girdle and swung herself over the edge and onto the steep walkway.

With her left hand firmly gripping the torch and her right holding onto the outcropping rocks on the wall of the cavern, Rose began her descent. The stone ledge beneath her feet was smooth and must have been worn down by some ancient flood, but there were little piles of gravel here and there that several times caused her to slide and almost lose her balance. *Careful, careful,* she reminded herself. *If you fall or lose the torch, you will be of no use to Derry.* At last she reached the flat surface of the bridge and dreaded what she knew she must do next. Taking a deep breath she held out her torch and peered down into the pit below. A scream echoed around and around her, and she realized it was her own voice as she stared down at the crumpled form which lay below. There some thirty feet below her, Sybil lay twisted and still. Something red gleamed in the torchlight. At first she thought it was Sybil's red hair, but then she recognized the ruby broach. There was no movement. Rose was certain the maidservant was dead.

"God help me, God help me," Rose whispered as she held her torch over the other side of the bridge, searching for Derry. "Thank you, Lord, thank you!" she exclaimed as she saw nothing but rock and stone. *Then Derry hadn't fallen with Sybil.* "Where is my son?" Rose shouted down to her dead servant. "What have you done with him?" Her questions echoed around and around, and as they died out she was left alone in the silent cavern.

Chapter Eighteen

ROSE FORCED HERSELF to stand still. She tried to pray but could only utter one word over and over, "Peace—peace—peace." And just as the Lord had stilled the tossing sea with that word, so now He calmed her with His peace. She looked straight ahead and saw at the end of the bridge a narrow opening into a tunnel. At the foot of the opening lay an extinguished torch. She bent down and picked it up. *Sybil's torch must have gone out and she must have slipped as she tried to cross the bridge in the darkness. But that means she must have left Derry alone somewhere at the end of this tunnel.* Rose took a deep breath and stepped through the opening.

As the tunnel descended it grew lighter and when it turned sharply to the left, she could see a large chamber beyond, which was suffused with gray light. Sunlight filtered in through an opening in the high vaulted ceiling of the cavern. She heard the sound of running water and could distinguish an underground stream which had cut a channel through the center of the chamber. As her eyes adjusted to the dim light, there was no need for her to keep the torch burning to see here, but she knew she would need its light for her retreat lest Sybil's fate befall her.

On the opposite side of the stream, the floor of the cave was uneven. A large wall of rocks obscured her view of its far recesses. So she kept to her side of the stream, carefully stepping over several wide gashes in the stony floor.

As she passed the wall of rocks, the stream spilled over a large rock into a stony basin about six feet across. The stream had been but a thin trickle of water, but now it began to gush into the stagnant pool of water. The heavy rains were beginning to feed the stream. She saw that the pool would have to fill to several more feet before the water spilled over into a smaller basin and ran down its narrow channel to the far end of the cavern.

Directly across from her, on the other side of the pool, was a wide table-like stone. At first glance there appeared to be a small rock resting on it, but as she leaned over the basin and peered at the object, her heart jumped. It was a chunk of bread. This must be the site of Sybil's camp. "Derry! Derry!" Rose called frantically, forgetting for the moment that her son could not hear. She raised her torch high above her head, straining to see to the far wall of the cavern. There were several large rocks farther back from the stone table, so she began to walk past the basin, searching for a safe place to cross the stream so she could investigate.

As she turned she saw out of the corner of her eye something white flash. She turned and looked across the pool. Derry! Still clad in his little white nightshirt, he was peering from behind one of the large rocks. His smudged face was streaked with tears and from his left wrist dangled a strip of green cloth. Sybil had been wearing a green gown. *Evidently, thought Rose, the maid had tied him to keep him from wandering off while she went to get more food.*

For a moment, Derry stared at her with blank, frightened eyes. Then he seemed to recognize her and his face screwed up into a look of abject grief. He whimpered and toddled toward her.

She held up her hand. "Stay, dearling. Mama will come to you. Here, let me just find a place to—Derry!" He was at the edge of the basin now, sobbing loudly and holding his arms out to her. "Don't fall!" She dropped the torch and jumped into the pool as Derry stepped off the edge and tumbled toward the water. The swirling water weighted down her skirts, but she lunged forward with all her might and managed to break his fall. The pool was about two feet deep now and they were both submerged for a few seconds, but she had a firm hold on his nightshirt and, pulling herself to the edge, she lifted him up in her arms. "There, there. Mother has you now." She patted him reassuringly and he threw his arms around her neck and clung to her.

She saw that her torch had gone out when she dropped it and felt a rise of panic. She dare not try to leave the cavern without a light. *Ah, well*, she thought, *if we stay a whole day in this cave before we are discovered, at least I've found my son.* With Derry clinging to her and the water swirling, it took Rose some time to stand to her feet, for the bottom of the pool was as slick as ice. Shifting Derry's weight she decided to take one large stride and place him on the opposite bank while she pulled herself up. As she stepped down she felt her right foot slide down into a narrow fissure. She cried out as a sharp pain shot up her leg. Derry became frightened and squirmed in her arms, causing her to fall backward into the water, feeling at the same time an awful crunch in her ankle. They were both submerged again but despite the pain she gripped him firmly with one hand and pushed herself to an upright sitting position.

The water was coming up to her neck and she had to lift Derry so his head was above water. He sputtered and choked and stamped on her legs, causing even more agony to her injured foot. As the water level reached her chin, she made one great effort to free her foot, but the pain almost caused her to black out and the weight of her wet clothes and Derry's shifting form were too much to fight. "Dear God, dear God, what can I do?" *If only I were able to stand and throw him up to the bank. But in his panic he might tumble back into the water again and I couldn't move to help him.*

As the water crept still higher, she took one last gulp of air and held Derry to her tightly. Then with all her strength she placed her hands under his arms and thrust him out of the water as high as her arms could reach. He grew limp as she did, but she knew he could breathe, for his head was well above the rim of the basin. He must have fainted from fright and exhaustion. *Just as well, just as well,* she thought. *He will not struggle and go under any sooner that way.* She locked her arms. *Strong as an oak, strong as an oak. Here, Father, he's yours. I can do no more than hold him up until I perish. Take him, dear Lord.*

The seconds passed and she fought the tremendous urge to exhale. *Why should I not?* she thought. *'Twill end it all quickly. Nay, I'll fight to keep him alive until the last moment.* After about a minute had passed, her lungs relaxed a bit and she felt as if she could hold her breath forever. She opened her eyes and saw not darkness but a lovely yellow glow.

Suddenly she felt Derry wrenched from her grasp, but she was not afraid. *An angel has carried Derry up to heaven, and he's placing him in the gentle arms of Jesus,* she thought dreamily.

"Rose, Rose."

Why, now she was on Boxton green. She was wearing her blue silk gown and through the yellow haze of sunset Thomas was riding toward her. How handsome he looked as he dismounted and walked toward her, calling her name. Pain surged through her leg and enveloped her.

She heard someone coughing and retching. *Poor soul, who can that be?* Then she realized it was herself. She lay back on something hard and cold and opened her eyes.

"My love, my love, are you all right?"

It was Thomas. He was hovering over her anxiously. *He looks older,* she thought vaguely. *Why is this grass so hard beneath me?*

"Dearling, can't you hear me?" he asked and gently shook her shoulders.

Derry. She tossed her head from side to side and tried to sit up, but it only produced more pain in her leg and another fit of coughing. Thomas cradled her head in his arms and when she grew still, he stroked her hair and said, "Derry is safe, he's well. Humfrey has carried him home to Anne's care and will return with a wagon for you." She clutched at his arm. "Trust me, my love. He's alive. I swear it. We plucked the both of you out of the pool just in time."

"Praise God," Rose whispered.

"You can be grateful you were unconscious, for I had to hold you upright while Humfrey went underwater to force your foot out of the fissure. We must have returned to the manor soon after you left. Tad guided us here, and it was he who scampered through the chambers, leading us down to the pool."

"Sybil?"

"Aye, we saw her body. She must have waited until Derry fell asleep to go looking for food and slipped—"

Rose moaned with pain.

"My poor whiting. I'm afraid your ankle is broken, but it is a clean break. Humfrey is bringing wood for splints and leaves of the boneset plant to pack around your injury. He bent down and kissed her. "Close your eyes and try to rest. All is well. All is well."

Chapter Nineteen

"MAMA, COME SEE," said Derry as he pulled at her arm.

"One, moment, dearling," Rose answered. "Please wait outside." He smiled at her and then skipped on out into the courtyard.

"Truly a marvel," said Rose's guest. She was a young woman, simply dressed in a woolen gown and a plain white cap. Seated on her lap was a little girl, about four years old who squirmed and tried to get out of her mother's grasp. The young woman looked embarrassed as she struggled with the child. "Mistress Stratton, do you think my Mary can be taught to speak?"

"We can try, my dear," replied Rose, "and mayhap teach her to read lips."

"Your son, he seems so—well, just like any other eight-year-old child. I pray that Mary can learn to act as normal."

Rose thumped her cane on the floor with such force that her guest jumped. "Mistress Johnson," Rose began, "your daughter is deaf. If you want her to be placed in my school merely because you're ashamed of her affliction and desire her to act 'normal' so you won't be embarrassed, then I cannot help you." She stood up and leaned on her cane. "As you see, I am lame. A broken bone didn't mend properly and I will always have a weakness in my limb. But although I shall remain lame, this cane enables me to get about. It will not enable me to run, but I can walk. Using the methods of teaching the deaf which I acquired from a Spanish monk and from my own deductions, I cannot ever replace your child's own damaged hearing,

155

but I can help her to live among the hearing. Do you understand me?"

Mistress Johnson nodded and then burst into tears. "I did not mean—I love my little girl. It just breaks my heart to see her struggle and—"

Rose's face softened and she limped over to the young mother. "I know, my dear. Oh, how I do know!" She held out her hand. "Now dry your tears and bring little Mary outside." She led them out into the garden where Anne was overseeing a group of twelve children of varying ages. They were standing in a circle on the grass, playing a game of dodge ball. Derry was in the middle. He looked up as Rose approached and waved, just as the large inflated leather ball hit him lightly in the knee. He and all the other children laughed. Little Mary wiggled out of her mother's arms and ran to join them.

"Anne," Rose called, " 'tis about the children's rest time. Take Mistress Johnson up to the dormitory with you so that she can see the children's living quarters. After you come down, Mistress Johnson, we'll discuss your daughter." She put her arm around the other woman. "We'll do all we can to help your child. The most important thing you must do is to love her, love her just the way she is and know that God loves the both of you with an everlasting love."

She watched the two women and the children go off to the dormitory. *I must find another assistant soon,* she thought. *I'm so pleased that Anne and Robert Gilbert are going to wed. They are a perfect match for each other. She has enough practical wisdom to offset his head-in-the-clouds theology.*

Rose walked slowly up the drive to the entrance gate. *Thomas should be arriving this afternoon. I hope he is able to bring that little orphan he's found. Poor little scamp. Deaf and alone on the streets of London. No wonder he was caught stealing bread.*

She gazed down the road. *I suppose I shall always spend much time keeping watch at this gate, seeing Thomas off on his travels and awaiting his return. But he loves his work and I love mine and the times we spend together are precious indeed. I cannot wait to show him the workshop Humfrey has constructed for the older children. Dear Thomas. I couldn't ask for a kinder, more generous husband.* She limped to the massive iron gate and, taking her handkerchief, polished the small brass sign which hung from it. *And this,* she thought, *this is truly his most magnificent gesture.*

The sign was inscribed: The Derick Haler Memorial School for Deaf Children. She touched the name. *Ah, Derick, my first love, you prayed that God would take care of us, Derry and me—and He is. Aye, my love, He still is.*

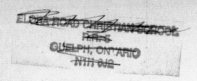